## "Josh, what if someone comes in?"

"We're only slow dancing," he murmured, pressing her against the wall on the dark side of the room. "What is it about you that has this effect on me?" His tongue touched Lauren's earlobe and she closed her eyes. Heat shot through her.

"My razor-sharp intellect?"

"Mmm. That'll do for a start."

If it were possible for a man to seduce and worship at the same time, Josh was doing it.

When one hand slid up and cupped her breast, she was ready to erupt. She was so ready, in fact, that if he even—

His other hand slid under the hem of her short black chiffon skirt. He touched her thigh, then caressed her bare bottom. "A thong." His voice held pleased discovery. "What color?"

"Peach," she managed to say. "Josh, someone's going to come…"

"I certainly hope so."

Dear Reader,

Writers are notorious for picking bits and pieces from people, news, events and their own experiences and turning them into stories. So when three writers get together to pack a whole lot of ideas into a miniseries—look out! I hope you enjoy the LOCK & KEY trilogy!

It was a blast working with Jamie Denton and Carrie Alexander to come up with three heroines who overcame their beginnings to unlock their own possibilities. It took some doing to imagine heroes who could give Mikki, Lauren and Rory a run for their money— but imagining sexy, no-holds-barred men who are a worthy match for our heroines is half the fun of writing for Harlequin Blaze.

I learned a lot about collaboration during this project. Writing can often be a solitary pursuit, but in this case it was more like an online party as we wove story threads and compared notes and talked over scenes from three (or six!) different points of view. The result was a strengthened bond between me and my sister writers—and, I hope, three stories you'll remember for a long time.

Drop by my Web site, www.shannonhollis.com, to see what's coming up next....

Warmly,

*Shannon Hollis*

## Books by Shannon Hollis

**HARLEQUIN BLAZE**
144—HIS HOT NUMBER

**HARLEQUIN TEMPTATION**
931—HER PRIVATE EYE

# *On the Loose*
# SHANNON HOLLIS

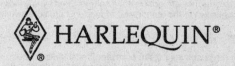

# HARLEQUIN®

TORONTO • NEW YORK • LONDON
AMSTERDAM • PARIS • SYDNEY • HAMBURG
STOCKHOLM • ATHENS • TOKYO • MILAN • MADRID
PRAGUE • WARSAW • BUDAPEST • AUCKLAND

ISBN 0-373-79174-7

ON THE LOOSE

Dear Reader,

*An Evening To Remember...* Those words evoke all kinds of emotions and memories. How do you plan a romantic evening with your guy that will help you get in touch with each other on every level?

Start with a great dinner that you cook together. Be sure to light several candles and put fresh flowers on the table. Enjoy a few glasses of wine and pick out your favorite music to set the mood. After dinner take the time to really talk to each other. Hold hands and snuggle on the sofa in front of the fireplace. And maybe take a few minutes to read aloud selected sexy scenes from your favorite Harlequin Blaze novel. After that, anything can happen....

That's just one way to have an evening to remember. There are so many more. Write and tell us how you keep the spark in your relationship. And don't forget to check out our Web site at www.eHarlequin.com.

Sincerely,

Birgit Davis-Todd
Executive Editor

For Jamie and Carrie, with thanks,
and to Jen, for inviting me to the party

Acknowledgments

I'd like to thank Karina
for her knowledge of modern Chinese-American life and
for the correct way to make shui jao. Thank you, Maddie,
for your sense of humor and Lorelei's tag lines.
And thank you, Lynn and Karen, for all the work
and love you pour into enabling our habit over at IBD.

Do you have your tickets yet for the Baxter House benefit? If not, better hurry. The buzz around town is that this is the "don't miss" party this spring. Think women with locks and men with keys. Think Deerfield Jewelers, ladies. Think prizes up the wazoo—donated by restaurants, wineries and theaters from here to Mendocino—for every couple whose lock and key is a match.

I won't even go into what else you might find a match for. There's a reason the tagline is "Unlock the possibilities," know what I mean? Use your imaginations!

While you're doing that, think about the cause. Your ticket price goes straight to the building fund for Baxter House, a transitional home for girls coming out of the foster care system. This is social worker and activist Maureen Baxter's pet project, and now she's made it ours. She's made it fun.

Deerfield white gold, girls. What's not to like?

Lorelei

# 1

"THE NEXT TIME I get the urge for something hot and hard between my legs, I'm going to buy a motorcycle."

Lauren Massey tossed back the last of the White Knight in her glass and considered heading to the bar for another, then decided against it. The crowd waiting for drinks was four people deep, and besides, she was supposed to be snagging interviews for a story for her column. With two drinks in a row, she'd be more likely to giggle or flirt rather than ask meaningful questions...or ask questions way too personal to put into print.

Her column, "Lorelei on the Loose," ran in a paper called *San Francisco Inside Out*, a left-wing cross between for-real street reporting and the tabloids you got at the checkout counter. Oh, they didn't report on alien babies and celebrity divorces—unless the celebrities were local or the aliens had agreed to appear on the Channel 4 News. *Inside Out* was about entertainment, with a little activism thrown in, and for now, it paid the bills.

In the snarky, no-holds-barred persona of Lorelei, Lauren also ran a Web log, or "blog," connected to *Inside Out*'s Web site, where she commented live on everything from clothes to politics to local charity events like this one. Her identity was a secret closely guarded by the paper, partly because she had a knack for stirring up controversy and partly because readers couldn't resist a mystery and were always trying to guess who she was. They also couldn't resist writing in and taking her on in public, which meant that Lorelei got the highest number of hits on the *Inside Out* site. You'd think this would make the Queen of Pain give her a raise, but it just made her managing editor demand more content, more trend-setting commentary, more everything.

So, like any good columnist, tonight Lauren was going to be multitasking—doing her part for charity and hunting a story like a basset hound.

"A vibrator's cheaper." Lauren's foster sister, Aurora "Rory" Constable, was still smiling over her motorcycle crack. Lauren glanced at the drink on the table in front of her, illuminated by a little Victorian lamp that tried to compete with the colored spotlights and the glittering bling-bling of the twentysomething crowd all around them. Rory would nurse her drink for the next hour on the principle that the calories in it would get burned off in proportion to her activity— which, at this charity event disguised as a key party, could amount to anything from casual conversation to sex in the broom closet.

"A vibrator doesn't have that 'mess with me and I'll kick your butt' appeal," Lauren pointed out.

"Bad date, sweetie?" Michaela Correlli, the middle of the three foster sisters, slid an arm around Lauren's shoulders and gave her a quick hug. She was also the clever so-and-so who had slipped Lauren an éclair during their regular Saturday-morning gabfest at Lavender Field last week and who, when her defenses were down, had talked her into coming tonight.

To survive in the foster care system, Lauren had

learned that when life tossed you a lemon, you made lemon chiffon pie and invited other people to eat it. So, even though a key party wasn't her usual scene, she could use it to further her career and to help out a good cause at the same time. But she was the lucky one. Poor Rory had had less than a week to come up with the donation of baked goods for five-hundred-plus people that Mikki had recklessly promised on her behalf in exchange for the tickets. It was a good thing Rory's staff at Lavender Field, her chain of bakeries, all possessed the California attitude that considered goodies for five hundred a "challenge," never a problem.

Mikki was good at talking people into challenges. Nobody messed with her. In high school, nobody had messed with Lauren, either, once they'd found out Michaela was her foster sister. Even now, after one look from those merciless blue eyes, deputy D.A.s and social workers alike dropped to their knees, begging.

For a lot of things.

"The worst," Lauren replied over the canned pop music that was playing until the band was ready to start. "Remember that really sweet guy I met online about four months ago? The wealth-planning advisor?"

"Didn't you show us some of his messages?" Rory asked. "And his picture? I thought he looked nice."

"Oh, he is nice," Lauren assured them. "His mom told me so during our date."

Mikki set her diet soda on the table with a clank. "You're at the meet-the-parents stage already? Is there something you didn't tell us about this guy? Should we be looking at poufy pink bridesmaid dresses?"

"God forbid. There's a lot of stuff he didn't tell me." Lauren glanced longingly at the bar again, then back to her sisters. "Such as the fact that he isn't a wealth planner at all. He's a finance major at San Francisco State and a permanent student. As in thirty and still living with his mom."

"So how did she get into this?" Rory wanted to know.

"He brought her on our date. In fact, she was a lot more interesting than he turned out to be. He writes beautiful e-mails, but in person?" Lauren waved her hand, shooing away the memory of her brief foray into online relationships that had started out as research for a story and had ended as…well, as dinner with an entertaining fifty-year-old archaeologist. Oh, yeah, and her son.

"As of tonight, I'm going to be like you, Mikki. I'm putting men on hold and focusing on important stuff, like nailing down this story."

It was clear Michaela was trying not to laugh at the sad state of her love life. "Are you sure you want to do that?" She fingered the white-gold locket on the chain around her neck, a little suitcase-shaped charm identical to the ones worn by Lauren and Rory and half the crowd at this fund-raiser. "What if Johnny Depp shows up with the key to your suitcase and you win the getaway for two?"

"He wasn't invited. But even if he was, I'd swap with you and you could have him, Mikki Mantis. I'm here to mingle and interview people. That's all."

Mikki swatted her on the arm for using the nickname she hated, and while Lauren got the last laugh on her sister, Maureen Baxter pushed aside a burgundy-velvet curtain and grabbed the microphone. The music faded and when she said, "Welcome to Clementine's, everyone," the noise level in the crowded club dropped by a couple of decibels. "I'm Maureen Baxter and I'm your hostess this evening."

She paused while the crowd hooted and whistled. Maureen knew everybody here, and if she didn't know you, she had a contact who did. Tall and elegant, with dark hair cut in a bob, her taupe chiffon gown hugged her curves and its sequins caught the spotlights trained on the stage. Mikki and Rory both knew her better than Lauren did. Maureen, too, had been one of the kids at the old house on Garrison Street where Emma Constable, Rory's real mother and Lauren's and Mikki's foster mom, took in the teenage hard cases from the foster care system.

Where Lauren had finally found her mismatched but true family.

"You're probably wondering what the deal is with the keys and lockets you were given at the door. Well, here's how it works. All the men have keys. All the women have locked suitcase charms." Maureen dropped her voice. "Yes, girls, these are white gold, from Deerfield, and we get to keep 'em." More hooting and some applause. "Guys, your job is to find the woman whose lock fits your key—and I mean that strictly in the practical sense. Every couple who gets a match gets a prize and a chance at the grand prize for tonight's charity event—a getaway for two. Best of all, you get to meet new people and have some fun."

Cheering from the crowd. Maureen waved a hand for quiet.

"And let's not forget why we're really here. Tonight's event is incredibly important to me because it will make the building fund for Baxter House healthy again. So far we have the land, which I inherited, the planning cycle is complete, the foundation has been poured and a couple of contractors—among them a wonderful guy who is actually here tonight—have donated their services."

Lauren glanced at Mikki and Rory and made an "I'm impressed" face.

"Good on you, Maureen," Mikki said in the direction of the stage, then turned to her sisters. "With land at a premium around here and contractors booked a year in advance, you've gotta believe she worked her butt off for this."

"I wonder who the guy is?" Rory said.

"Our little suitcase charms mean something, as anyone who has ever been in the foster care system knows," Maureen went on. "Sometimes all you have is what fits in a single duffel bag. Your whole life, all your memories, everything that is unique to you, stuffed inside a single suitcase. Some of you here know what I'm talking about."

The three women glanced at each other again. Some kids came with a lot of stuff. Some came with nothing. Lauren had been one of the one-bag kids—a gangly fifteen-year-old with nothing to her name but a picture of herself as a baby with her parents, a pair of jeans and a couple of T-shirts and a battered copy of the *Norton Anthology of English Literature* that she'd lifted from her last school.

Mikki's face told her she remembered the same thing and she slid an arm around Lauren's shoulders.

"Your fifty-dollar cover is not paying for the club or media coverage," Maureen assured them. "It's going toward the building fund, to purchase rebar and beams and drywall. This may not seem very glamorous, but I can't tell you how much it will mean to an eighteen-year-old girl who has just been released from the system and has no idea how to go about starting her life other than taking it to the streets. Baxter House will mean a new start for that girl, and I'm grateful to each of you for coming out to support it."

Maureen grinned at the crowd and waved behind her at the band, who had been quietly filing onto the stage while she was talking. "But now, we're going to have fun. So go out, find your key partner and have a good time!"

The band launched into a dance number with a great beat and Lauren's foot began to tap. Somewhere in the crowded club was a person who had the key that fit her locked charm, but Lauren just couldn't bring herself to go from person to person, allowing them to try out their keys. Some were having a lot of fun with it. She had work to do.

And she'd better get on with it.

She leaned over to Rory. "I'm going to go talk to people. Are you going to see what's going on in the kitchen?"

Lavender Field specialized in a dazzling array of breads, rolls and other sinful things. They were so good that rumor had it you could tell how well a company treated its employees simply by the presence of a box with the green-and-lavender logo in the coffee room.

White-gold charms and rolls and pastries from Lavender Field? Maureen knew how to treat her guests— and potential contributors to her project.

Rory tossed back the last of her drink and draped her lavender shawl over the back of her chair. "Hell, no. I'm going to dance."

Lauren watched her sister tap someone on the shoulder and, on the pretext of trying out the man's key, invite him to dance. The light from a gold spotlight slid over Rory's graceful, generous body as she passed under it, and then she and her partner disappeared into the crowd on the black-and-white-checkered dance floor.

Music blasted from the stage, lights flashed and swooped, and from somewhere in the back, a woman screamed with laughter. People laughed and talked over the beat as they danced, the whole crowd bobbing up and down in time with the music.

Lauren scanned the room for her first victim.

She'd already picked Maureen's brain about the background of the key party and the logistics of setting one up. A woman as driven for her cause as Maureen was didn't waste her time on angles that didn't succeed—and a key party was pretty much guaranteed to succeed. But what Lauren needed was the voice on the street who, let's face it, came to these things not because they were as passionate about the cause, but because deep down they believed—hoped—they'd find true love.

Or at least a date for the evening.

She zeroed in on an Asian girl in turquoise silk sitting in one of the dining alcoves, partially hidden by sound-absorbing velvet drapes. She blinked as the girl turned her head and she recognized the glossy fall of blue-black hair and the sloe eyes of her own roommate. Well, why not? Vivien's opinions were as valuable as those of a stranger, and it was an easy way to start.

"Sorry, I'm straight," Vivien Li deadpanned as Lauren slid in beside her on the padded leather-look bench.

"Sure, you are. You're not getting away from me that easily." Lauren grinned. "Nice dress, by the way. You didn't tell me you were coming to this shindig."

She and Vivien had been roommates since their junior year at Berkeley. Once they'd graduated—Lauren with a degree in communications and Viv with one in computer electronics—both of them had concluded there was no reason to give up a comfortable living arrangement. Besides, Lauren often thought, what sane woman would let go of a roomie who could cook as well as Viv did? So they'd moved across the Bay and Lauren had gone to work while Viv slaved at her post-grad degree and worked part-time to pay her half of the rent.

"Someone at work couldn't go at the last minute, so he gave me his ticket. It said 'Unlock the Possibilities.' What does that mean, exactly?"

Lauren laughed. "That's what I'm trying to find out. How about I interview you for *Inside Out?*" She took her minirecorder out of her evening bag, turned it on and put it on the table between them, next to the red glass lamp with dangling crystals that propped up the wine list.

"How come I always have to be your lab rat?" Viv complained. "You know 'Lorelei' scares me silly. I always picture her looking like Cruella De Vil. The cartoon one, not Glenn Close."

Lauren shook her head. "Nope. She looks like Alicia Silverstone crossed with Maggie Gyllenhaal in *Secretary.*"

"Ai-ya," Vivien moaned. "A demented blonde who wants to pick my brain. And probably eat it."

"No, that would be the Queen of Pain. To her, the word *freelancer* has no meaning. Every time I go into the office she has her people locked up in meetings, and she tries to suck me into the vortex with them."

Other than having to endure her editor, working on the Lorelei column and blog for *Inside Out* was fun. And a regular paycheck, no matter what its size, was nice, too. Realistically, Lauren knew blogging was a phase that, like Bennifer and platform shoes, wouldn't last. What she really wanted to do was to work for a high-profile magazine, and not just as a contributing freelancer, either. Someday she'd be on the staff at *Left Coast,* which was based here in San Francisco and ran the kinds of stories that were nominated for major literary prizes.

However, "Lorelei" wasn't going to get her noticed there. In fact, she was probably more of a liability than an asset. But her press pass got her into more events than not, and it all gave her material she could use.

"I need some insight into this whole key thing," Lauren said. "I value your opinions. Besides, you're in my demographic."

"What's that? Lesbian Chinese-American master's candidates?"

"No. Singles. It's a very broad demographic. So, what brought you out tonight besides the fund-raiser? What's the attraction in it?"

Vivien considered the question. "It's more personal than want ads and doesn't have the commitment factor of dinner and a movie, you know?"

"Commitment factor?"

"Yeah. Do I sleep with her because she had to pre-order the duck à l'orange? Or did we go to Korean barbecue when I was expecting the Top of the Mark, so all she gets is a kiss and some garlic breath? With a key party, you don't have to ask yourself questions like this. Your key fits, you like the person, you hang around and talk for a while."

"What if you don't like the person? What if they have garlic breath?"

"Then you go put your ticket in the prize-drawing thing, slip them a mint and move on. Everyone knows the drill, so there's no hard feelings."

"It's like a giant mixer."

Viv nodded. "Only cooler."

Lauren turned off the recorder. Cool was good. *Inside Out* liked cool, though *Left Coast* would probably turn up its nose at it. "Thanks for the insight."

"Mind you, this event is set up for hetero mixing," Viv said. "I have to work a little harder."

Lauren looked out over the twisting, laughing crowd. "What you do is swap your lock for a gay guy's key. That way both of you are lined up to get the right partner."

"Oh-oh." Viv's face, a perfect oval with the kind of fine complexion that needed no makeup, brightened. "Good plan. I'm all over it." She leaned over and gave Lauren an affectionate peck. "Gotta go unlock some possibilities."

Lauren followed her out into the crowd and, for the next forty-five minutes, did her best to circulate and talk to people.

"Mind if I try you on for size?"

Oh, please. She'd heard at least five versions of *that* one. Lauren pasted on a polite smile and turned to the man—well, kid, really—in the scuffed leather jacket and presented her chest to him. Just how many variations of "I'll show you mine if you show me yours" could people come up with? By the end of the evening the odds were good she'd find out.

The backs of the kid's fingers brushed the peach silk of her tank top as he lifted the tiny suitcase. He jumped. She didn't. Lauren gazed at him thoughtfully as he flourished his little key and tried to fit it into the lock. He looked familiar. Where had she seen him before?

Her lock didn't open.

Oh, good.

"Nice to have met you," the guy said cheerfully, obviously not that cut up that he wasn't going to be spending the rest of the evening with her. He moved on to Rory, who was standing ten feet away. She topped him by a couple of inches, but he, evidently, was a brave man. He reached for her cleavage.

Lauren looked out over the crowded dance floor. The guy was in her reader demographic. She should have interviewed him while she'd had the chance. But she'd already talked to six or seven people and so far hadn't found one who presented an opposing view. Everybody seemed to think a key party was a good thing. But then, if you hated them you'd probably just put a check in the mail to Maureen's office, wouldn't you?

She glanced around the room in an attempt to locate Michaela, who had gone to get more drinks. Those who had found the person with the key to their suitcase were crowding the stage, where Maureen was busy handing out prizes and putting the numbered slips from the lockets into a big rotating basket like the ones the lotteries used.

Lauren moved her stool closer to Rory's when her sister sat down. "Is there a reason that kid looked familiar?"

Rory always knew stuff like this. A woman who had subscriptions to *People* and *Variety* and who hosted movie-and-dinner parties where people actually came in costume had to know.

*"Alien Bodyguard."*

Lauren snapped her fingers. "That's it." He'd played the hapless younger brother killed off on the first episode of *Alien Bodyguard,* one of the midseason TV shows Lorelei had ripped to shreds. That had started a lovely big controversy about turning science fiction novels into TV shows that had made her blog traffic peak at ten thousand hits a day. She'd better go interview him before his key fit someone's lock. A celebrity quote wasn't something you lucked onto every day.

"No sign of Johnny Depp?" Michaela swiveled around a good-looking jerk who was making graphic hand motions and put their drinks on the table, including a soft drink for herself.

*Good girl, Mikki.* Every time her sister resisted temptation meant a victory in a long chain of victories that took her further away from the alcoholic darkness of four years ago, which had peaked after her breakup with her husband.

They chatted for a few minutes and then Lauren said, "Why do they pair the women up with men, anyway? My perfect date is a little old lady with an early bedtime." She scanned the room for a leather jacket. "Then I could go home and start on this story."

Michaela bumped her shoulder as she sat. "Don't be so focused, honey. Have some fun with this. Your partner could be tall, rich and gorgeous."

"I hope he's tall, rich and gay, and I can give his key to Vivien. Don't forget, I'm in the market for a motorcycle, not a man."

"What about the fun part? You're like a laser beam, tracking your target." Mikki looked half-amused, half-exasperated. "Come on. Let's get out there and dance."

But before Lauren could reply, Rory nudged Michaela and her sister froze at the sight of a man approaching them.

"Oh, my God," Lauren murmured. As if her thoughts had conjured him up, Mikki's ex, Nolan Baylor, approached them with those bedroom eyes and that same confident grin, both trained on her sister. But how could this be? Wasn't his law practice in Los Angeles? What was he doing here, looking all buff and casual in his charcoal polo shirt? And what business did he have spoiling Mikki's night by showing up?

But as anyone in her family could tell you, Mikki Correlli could take care of herself. "What the hell are you doing here?" she snapped.

In answer, Nolan grinned and flourished a small, white-gold key.

# 2

LAUREN COULDN'T DECIDE whether to leap up and claw his eyes out, or let Michaela do it. Something seemed to combust in the air between her sister and former brother-in-law as he practically taunted her with the key. Her eyes flashing with anger and contempt, Michaela made a big show of ignoring him and introducing his friend, Tucker Schulz. Tuck's eyes signaled interest, but that was the last thing Lauren could deal with amid all this sudden tension. Her options seemed to be sticking by Mikki's side for support and fading into the wallpaper. Neither was very appealing.

Thank God there were no serious men in her past to reappear and mess up her life. She'd had enough trouble keeping it on an even keel on her own. After she'd come to live at Garrison Street, it had taken years for her to figure out that there were people in this world who would actually love you and stick around when you said you loved them. Her childhood had taught her the opposite, after Dad had taken off when she was ten. When she was fourteen, Mom had looked at the choice between her habit and her daughter—*heroin or the kid? Hmm, that's a hard one. Let's pick heroin.* And the choice had killed her.

That was why love—the kind of love that meant picket fences and permanence and kids—was one helluva scary proposition, one that both attracted and re-pelled Lauren.

Not that she was against picket fences in principle. She was looking thirty-one in the face, after all. But she seemed to have a knack for picking guys who already had something in their lives she had to compete with. Like Carl, who loved programming games for Lucas Arts more than doing things with her. Or Luis, who had wanted kids and picket fences as long as his mom and most of his extended family could come and share them, too.

Then she'd gone out on a limb and tried online dat-ing with one of those nifty interfaces where you filled out your wish list of the perfect man's qualifications. What had she wound up with?

An interesting archaeologist—oh, yeah, and her son.

Feeling like a coward, Lauren excused herself as gracefully as she could and got back to work. Circling the room, she ran a hand over the mass of curls Rory's clever fingers had coaxed into her taffy-colored mop, and got her mind back on a safer track.

She needed to decide on a theme for her article. What did it say about society when you could surf for a part-ner in the same way she surfed TV channels, searching for something that looked good enough to spend some time on?

Hmm. That would make a good lead. Then she could follow it with—

"Excuse me," said a baritone voice behind her. She turned and looked straight into a crisp shirtfront. Her gaze traveled up a row of buttons, one by one. Here was the stuff dreams were made on, or it would be if her sub-conscious ever thought to cast men like this.

His hair, which was on the long side, flopped into his

left eye in a way that should have made him look messy
but instead made him look intriguing and mysterious.
He grinned, and she dropped ten years from her first es-
timate. He had the kind of grin that made a woman do
a double take—all little-boy mischief on the one hand
and pure male appreciation on the other. What was it
about dimples in a male cheek that could make a woman's knees go all soft and wobbly? And check out the
way the overhead light made hollows under his cheekbones. His eyes were dark as sin, with long lashes that
managed to look sexy instead of feminine.

"May I?" He held up his key.

A miracle. No tired one-liner. The man was not only
yummy, he was so classy he'd achieved originality.

"Sure." She should be so lucky.

No, luck was a lady tonight. An old lady with an
early bedtime. A frisson of sensation tiptoed across her
skin as his long, sensitive fingers brushed the shallow
curves of her breasts. Not for the first time, she wished
she were a little deeper in the keel, like Rory. Enough
to make this charmer focus on her instead of on the little suitcase he held.

*Never mind, Cinderella. You're not at the ball to find*
*a prince. Not unless he's willing to give you a quote.*

He inserted his key in her lock and turned it.

*Snick.* The two halves of the suitcase sprang open the
way women probably welcomed him all the time.

Oh, my. Lauren hadn't been expecting anyone to open
her lock; she'd kept herself so focused on interviewing
people that she'd sidestepped most of the possibilities. It
was one thing to ogle this guy and appreciate him the way
she did good food and beautiful scenery. But now that he
had the key to her lock, she either had to let herself go
and enjoy whatever he had to offer, or—or what? Leave?

Suddenly escape looked much less appealing than it had a few minutes ago.

"I finally lucked out." He smiled down at her. "I have to admit I was here more for the benefit part than the key part. But now it looks as if the benefit is all mine."

"We'll have to see, won't we?" Lauren sounded a lot more casual than she felt as she fished out the paper slip her suitcase held. "We turn this little piece of paper in to Maureen and get a prize, then she enters us in the big drawing. But you go ahead. I have to talk to someone."

"Oh, no. We're in this together."

He offered her his hand and, instead of murmuring the excuse that fluttered on her tongue, she found herself taking it and allowing him to lead her to the stage. His fingers were warm and very sure as they wrapped around hers.

"I'm Josh, by the way." He glanced down at her, one eyebrow raised. She'd thought only English actors could pull off that lazy, inquiring brow. It managed to transmit both interest and inquiry in one movement.

Sigh. *No, you have to work tonight. Don't you?* "Lauren."

Since he was already holding her hand, he couldn't exactly shake it. He squeezed her fingers instead. He might have been about to say more, but behind a knot of people, Lauren caught a glimpse of the *Alien Bodyguard* kid's leather jacket. Aha!

"Josh, I don't mean to be rude, but I really do need to speak to someone." She tried to disengage her hand. The part of her that loved forties swing music and bought antique clothes wondered why she was giving up a chance with a gorgeous, interested man in favor of a kid who didn't even know who she was. "I'm a journalist, and I'm after that kid over there in the jacket."

"Kit Maddox? No problem, I'll wait."

What circles did he move in that he knew the actor's name? Maybe he was in the movie business. Maybe she should introduce him to Rory. But then, it was a safe bet he wouldn't be there when she got back. Mentally, she kissed the delectable Josh goodbye and headed off across the floor.

Five minutes and one dance later—did anyone have any idea how hard it was to hold a recorder while someone was dipping you?—she had her celebrity quote. Now she could go home and make Lorelei eat some crow in public about her treatment of *Alien Bodyguard,* and go into a snit about it, which would make people respond on the chat board, which would make traffic spike, which would make the Queen of Pain happy.

She detoured around a couple who looked as if they were doing gym exercises to "Hot, Hot, Hot," and found Josh standing right where she'd left him.

The impact hit her under the ribcage. Had he been watching her dance with Maddox? Had he liked what he'd seen? What presence the guy had. He stood there, one hip cocked and one hand in the pocket of his black jeans, in a pose straight out of *GQ* or *Esquire.*

The appealing thing was, he seemed to be completely unaware of both pose and the fact that women were ebbing and flowing around him like a crowd of interested muses. Lauren liked that in a man. Not that she thought everything should be all about her—except when it came to competing for the bathroom mirror.

He strolled over, parting the disarray with effortless ease. "I saw you caught Maddox. Did you get what you needed from him?"

He *had* been watching her, just the way she was

watching him. "Yes, and now I need something from you. How do you *do* that?"

He looked around, a charming little wrinkle between his brows. "Do what?"

She shook her head with a smile. "Never mind." If he didn't know the effect he had on women, all the better. Though why she was thinking about sharing the bathroom mirror at all was something she didn't want to go into at the moment.

"So tell me what you need from me," he said. "Before I make a few suggestions myself."

Lauren swallowed. His voice, even with a hint of a rasp around the edges, was as alluring as dark chocolate—and no doubt just as bad for you. But…her research was done and he was here and after all, it had been a long time since a man had looked at her like this.

"I need—" *I need you to go somewhere dark and quiet with me. I need you to unlock my possibilities.*

*No, you can't say things like that to a stranger. Mikki can, but not you.*

"I need you to give me an interview," she blurted. "I'm working on a piece about key parties and you're gorgeous. I mean, perfect. I mean, perfect for my demographic."

Oh, God, could she just die now and get it over with?

But when he threw back his head and laughed, she realized he wasn't laughing at her. He had the same kind of let-it-all-out humor that Emma Constable, her foster mother, possessed. The kind that attracted people to her the way people always walk to a fireplace when they enter a room.

"Is that all you want me for?" Josh said at last, when his amusement had simmered down to a smile. He smiled with his whole face, eyes included, which were crinkled at the corners. "I was hoping for a little more than that. Such as a prize. And a drink. And a dance, too. To start."

The smile took on another dimension, something hot and focused and filled with meaning.

*Whoa.* Lauren tried to take a breath and found she had to work at it. "Demanding, aren't you?"

"Not demanding." His eyes sparkled. "But when a woman tells me she needs me, I like to give her options."

Oh, there were definitely options here. Excitement and anticipation began to beat in her blood. "Why don't we start with the prize? That's the easy part."

"And the rest of it's hard?"

Lauren gave him a sideways glance as she led the way to the stage, a glance filled with humor and invitation. "That depends on you, doesn't it?"

He laughed again as they reached the podium. Maureen looked from Lauren to her companion and Lauren could swear the other woman physically restrained herself from reaching out and stroking him.

Lauren could hardly blame her, since she felt like doing that herself. Josh was incredibly touchable. The fabric of his shirt draped his shoulders and chest in a way that made you want to find out what was underneath. Most men wouldn't have worn black jeans to a semi-dressy event like this, but then, she didn't hear any of the women complaining about the way those jeans hugged him at thigh and hip. Or the way they accentuated his long stride.

Josh took the pair of tickets Maureen handed him and gave one to Lauren. *"Dancing in the Street."* He glanced at her. "I can't remember the last time I went to the theater. The way my work schedule has been, I think it was 1999."

Uh-oh. Shades of Carl the programmer.

The jungle beat of anticipation in Lauren's veins faded to a four-finger tap of disappointment. She knew the type—they romanced you just because they could, and then on Monday it was back to work in the corporate castle, where they felt safe and in control, and people were paid to do what they said, and they forgot to call.

Sure, he might be interested. God knew she was. But not enough to risk her self-esteem yet again with a guy who would put her on his scale of priorities somewhere between the office and his daily workout at the gym.

She needed to get out of this gracefully, with her pride still intact. Behind Josh's back, Lauren raked the sea of people with a hasty glance. Where were her sisters when she needed them?

GETTING THE LOVELY LAUREN to stay in one place long enough to talk to her was proving to be as difficult as pinning down George Lucas for an interview.

Josh had succeeded with Lucas, mind you, and the resulting story had been in the issue the magazine's readers had voted "Best of 2004." But so far tonight, all he'd managed with Lauren was to launch her at Kit Maddox—thereby losing a dance—and to win a theater ticket, after which she'd promptly vanished.

*So she's not interested. Write it off.*

That was the problem. He could swear she was interested. Part of it was the way she said outrageous things and then let her hazel eyes lock on his mouth while she waited for him to respond. Part of it was the way she'd looked at him after she'd come back from her dance with Kit Maddox—she'd lit up like a kid at

Christmas when she'd seen him waiting for her at the edge of the dance floor. It was pretty hard to resist a woman who looked at you like that.

Not that Josh had any intention of resisting. Until now he'd poured his concentration into work, into making enough money so that he'd finally feel safe. He had a knack for analyzing popular trends and seeing what consumers were going to need a few years down the line. That, combined with a business confidence that appealed to fellow venture capitalists, had made him a success in the oak-sheltered enclaves along Sand Hill Road in Silicon Valley.

However, it didn't do a damn thing for his social life. Which brought him back to this club and Maureen Baxter's charity bash. She was a friend of one of the other investors in *Left Coast* magazine, who had talked him into coming after the last quarterly forecast meeting. It hadn't taken much to convince him. It was time to put some serious investment into the opposite sex.

Both women and entertainment hadn't been on his agenda much in recent years. He was—he admitted it—rusty. He was going to change all that.

*Okay. But there are a lot of beautiful women here in short black skirts with fabulous legs. Pick one of them.*

*Nope,* he thought, obstinate even with the voice of reason in his head. *I have the key to Lauren's lock. That's supposed to mean something.*

The adventurer in him enjoyed a challenge. The logician figured the odds were pretty good she was as attracted to him as he was to her. And the male underneath it all wanted to know how those legs might feel wrapped around his waist, what that generous mouth would taste like under his, wanted to test the weight of those small breasts under her fragile silk top.

If things progressed that far. He was going to do everything in his power to see that they did.

Fifteen minutes later he found her sitting alone at a table near the dance floor, speaking rapidly into a mini-recorder. The music had slowed down, and colored spotlights circled the floor, illuminating her skin and then leaving her in the muted glow of the table lamp.

He folded himself into the spindly gilded chair next to her and waited for her to finish dictating her thought. "No rest for the published," he said, indicating the recorder.

She didn't apologize for losing him earlier. Nor did she look unhappy to see him. Either she had social Attention Deficit Disorder or she was focused in a major way on her story. He liked focus in a woman. But selfishly, he wanted that concentration turned on him for a little while.

"I still have what you need," he went on. "We haven't gotten around to that interview yet. Who do you write for?"

She put away the little unit in an evening bag that, from what he could see, didn't have room for much more than the recorder, a credit card and a lipstick. As she concentrated on the mundane task, her hair tumbled forward and hid most of her face. "I'm a freelancer. Anyone who will pay me, basically."

"I know how that goes," he said with sympathy. In his view, it wasn't important that he owned a thirty-three percent interest in the magazine. What mattered was the writing. He'd been submitting stories on spec since he'd been in high school, and his progress toward acceptances by *Left Coast* put him, in his opinion, at the top of his game. "Some months I could barely come up with the rent, much less pay the bills."

She shook her hair back. "Are you a journalist, too? I thought you might have been in the movie business."

He made a face. "Not me. The closest I get to movies is interviewing the odd producer or actor, which is why I knew Kit Maddox. No, I write for *Left Coast.*"

Something flashed in her eyes before her lashes came down and veiled them. "Lucky you. I'm not sure *Left Coast* is in the market for a piece on key parties."

"You wouldn't think so," he said easily. "Depends on the slant."

"Oh, come on. They only buy the kind of stuff that wins prizes. And I hardly think the Pulitzer panel would consider something like this."

From her tone, he couldn't tell whether that was a good thing or a bad one. "Well, I don't write my stuff with the Pulitzer committee's opinions in mind. Talk about a way to shut down your creativity."

To his relief, she smiled and the light came back into her face. For a moment suspended in time, he gazed at her. Her skin was smooth and tinted with color, her eyes the color of tea in the warm light from the lamp. Hair like spun taffy cascaded around her shoulders in an uncontrolled way that gave him an involuntary picture of how it would look tumbled on a pillow.

His pillow.

Tonight.

The band launched into the sensual, minor chords of an old blues song. At the same moment Lauren raised her gaze from where it had settled on his lips and met his eyes. He'd wanted that look turned on him. Oh, yes. Josh felt a shower of heat.

"Why did you run away from me?" he heard himself say.

The music wrapped around them, insinuating itself into his heartbeat, pulling them together. "Because you're a menace," she said softly.

A menace? Had he misheard her? He leaned in, close enough to hear. Close enough to smell her perfume. "How can that be?"

"The way chocolate is. The way it's so bad…and tastes so good." Her voice was low, her gaze locked on his mouth in a way that excited him past bearing.

"Would you like to dance?" His words came out involuntarily, a knee-jerk reaction to physical stimulus instead of the result of actual thought.

In response, she rose and held out her hand. He took it and led her onto the dance floor, feeling her fingers, cool and slender, in his. A pianist's hands. Or a journalist's, made for keyboarding. Touch typing.

Touching.

*Would you relax? It's just a dance. Keep this up and she'll have you arrested.*

She was too tall to fit under his chin, but she fit pretty nicely everywhere else. Her cheek brushed his as she settled into the rhythm of the music, their feet sliding into a lazy rhumba step.

"You've had some experience at this," he murmured into her hair, trying to make small talk while he got his equilibrium back.

"You like the way I move, do you?"

So much for small talk. In the space of eight words she turned the dance inside out so that all he sensed was the feel of her, the scent of her hair that combined something herbal with lemon, and the way her thighs brushed his with every step. He was pretty much in sensory overload, with no cycles left to initiate speech, so he settled for a noise in his throat that meant he agreed.

Yes, sir. His whole body agreed.

"I never thought of dancing as a social activity," she murmured. "Everyone should just admit that it's the opening act to something much more fun."

"Like what?" he managed to ask.

"I'll give you one guess." Her smile told him he wouldn't need more than that. But that smile, up close and personal, scrambled his brain.

*Get a grip. Maybe you're misreading her.* "An interview?"

She giggled against his shoulder and he closed his eyes in sheer pleasure at the movement of her breasts against his chest. So much for getting a grip. Try again.

"I'm still working on my original list. I've got the dance. We can have a drink afterward. And then it's up to you."

He hoped that she opted for "full speed ahead." His body, her body, the gypsy-blues music—all three combined in a heady mix that was going to set off fireworks any minute now.

Hell with it—maybe he should just think about getting Lauren out of here.

"About that interview," she murmured in his ear. Her lips moved against his earlobe and made desire spike through him. "I'm trying to think how I might describe you."

"Hardworking writer? Owns his own condo, paid off his car, definitely interested in the author of this piece. How's that?"

"Mmm, I was thinking of something more descriptive. Like a dark chocolate truffle. Sinful and rich and everything I know I shouldn't want, but that I crave."

She *craved* him? Josh gave up on trying to talk his body out of doing what it wanted to do when hers obviously wanted to do it, too. He glanced over the heads of the crowd. Where the hell was the door?

"I'm not sure I want you to think of me as food," he murmured. "Teeth are scary to a guy."

Again, her breasts bumped his chest gently as she muffled a laugh in his shoulder. And again, sparks of heat flared to life in his blood.

"I never use teeth on a truffle. I like to lick them on the outside until they melt. Then explore their lovely rich centers with my tongue."

*Breathe, before your lungs collapse.* "Suck them dry, do you?"

"Oh, yes," she purred in his ear. "And they love every minute of it."

Need sang through every vein and he forgot dance steps, propriety, everything but getting her alone. Then he remembered the private dining rooms, big enough for half a dozen—or two. With any luck, one of them would be empty. He slid his arm closer around her waist so that her hips ground against his and danced her over to the dark side of the room.

THE UNIVERSE WAS LAUGHING at her, Lauren thought, trying to talk sense to herself when her body and her runaway mouth definitely did not want to be sensible.

Yes, she was dancing to something very sexy and slow with a man who turned her knees to butter. Yes, her deprived libido had taken over and given him a shameless come-on.

She was behaving like the notorious Lorelei, the woman who chewed social commentary and pop culture for lunch, the woman the male sports writers loved to hate. Why, oh, why, did she have to be unlocked by a staff writer from *Left Coast* magazine, the very place she'd give her eye teeth to write for?

She'd laugh about this with Rory and Mikki tomorrow, over a latte and at least two of Rory's blueberry-cheese croissants. But for now she was going to steal these lovely moments and enjoy the heck out of them for as long as they lasted.

Because of course they wouldn't last. She couldn't afford to keep him around, looking gorgeous and sounding sinful and jeopardizing her career with every breath he took.

The music merged into something just as slow and sexy, some Latin love song that picked up where the gypsy blues left off. Josh's arm tightened around her and their haphazard direction took on purpose. Lauren brought her mind back from the hazy place where it was thinking about truffles and sex to the clear place where it thought about danger and realized that Josh had danced her into one of the club's private dining rooms.

"Now, then," he murmured, and pulled her flush against him. They might have had to be socially acceptable on the main dance floor, but in here, it appeared, all bets were off.

Yes, it was dangerous. But, oh, Lord, it felt so *good.* The two White Knights she'd consumed earlier had made her low opinions of key parties and her determination to work go all blurry and insubstantial. And who wanted opinions, anyway, when reality had eyes like this and a mouth to die for? What she wanted was Josh, and he was pressing against her at this moment as though he meant business. She slid her arms around him and let her body melt into the hardness of his.

Really hard.

Her knees, which had begun to get their strength

back, weakened as her body welcomed the bulge behind the button fly of those black jeans. Desire spangled her blood with tiny little rockets, all going off at once.

"Josh," she managed to get out, "what if someone comes in?"

"We're slow dancing," he murmured, his lips brushing her ear, his hips suggesting illicit things against hers. "Nothing wrong with that, is there?"

She shivered. If his mouth could make her body react like this when he spoke, what would happen if he actually kissed her? And those hips—they promised paradise. "Not as long as you stay between me and the door over there."

"What is it about you that has this effect on me?" he whispered. His tongue touched her earlobe and she closed her eyes as the little rockets went off again, trailing fire from her ear to her belly.

"My razor-sharp intellect?"

His hands slid over her skirt. "Mmm. That'll do for a start."

She couldn't stand it one more second. Leaning into him, she backed him against the wainscoting and took his mouth with hers.

He made a little sound of pure male pleasure in his throat and his lips opened. His mouth wooed, his tongue seduced and, before she knew it, it was she who was backed against the paneling, hanging on to him for dear life, because by God, if she let go she'd fall. She put everything she had into kissing him because he demanded no less.

Somehow he knew when to release her and let her breathe, dropping his lips to the neckline of her tank top and tracing kisses over her collarbone, working his way along her throat.

If it were possible for a man to seduce and worship at the same time, Josh was doing it.

When one hand slid up and cupped her breast, Lauren was sure she would come just from the fire of sensation in her nipple under his teasing thumb. She felt barely contained, ready to erupt. She was so ready, in fact, that if he even—

The other hand slid under the hem of her short, black chiffon skirt. Her thigh muscles, which under any other circumstances would have tightened in preparation for fending off the attack, relaxed and said, "Oh, yes."

"No stockings," he whispered in her ear, setting off a host of goose bumps. He touched her thigh, then cupped her bottom again, with no fabric between her skin and his bare hand this time. A brief exploration gave him his answer. "A thong." His voice held pleased discovery. "What color?"

What color? The color of flushed skin, the color of ripe fruit…oh, that was it. The color of her tank top.

"Peach," she managed to say.

"I love peaches." He slid one finger under it in back.

"Josh," she sighed, "someone's going to come…"

"I certainly hope so," he said, and slid the finger over her hip under the satiny cord, then down the front. His hand flattened against her pelvic bone while his finger found what it sought.

She moved her feet apart just enough to give him access and hung on as his finger slid into her folds, soft and swollen and wet, waiting for him. In three slow strokes he had her whimpering for release, and with one more it happened. An urgent orgasm exploded under that clever fingertip and spread through her belly, legs and all the way out to her fingers.

Silently she convulsed against the wall, head thrown back, body a river of sensation, while he dropped her skirt and pressed her against the wall in a hot, demanding kiss.

Seconds later Maureen Baxter walked in with half a dozen investors.

*From Lorelei's blog*

Before I went to the key party at Clementine's, I wasn't keen about just any random guy opening my lock. After all, how realistic is it to expect that you'd find the person who's right for you that way? The chances of winning the lottery are better. But now I'm reconsidering. The bash itself was a smashing success, and I don't just mean Baxter House, which now has enough in donations to commence building again. I mean that I met someone. Maybe it's only reasonable to expect the love of an evening. Or an hour. But, as the tag line on the tickets said, I unlocked a few possibilities, and for fifty bucks you can't ask for more than that.

For more on key parties, speed dating and other postmodern social customs, pick up *San Francisco Inside Out* and check out Lauren Massey's article in the Scene section. She was at Clementine's, too, in the company of the beautiful and scary Michaela Correlli, local child advocate, and the divine Aurora Constable, proprietor of Lavender Field. Did I mention the blueberry-cheese croissants?

Lorelei

# 3

AT THREE IN THE MORNING, Lauren uploaded "The Key to a Girl's Heart" to *Inside Out*'s FTP site so the production team could transfer it into layout for this week's issue. Lorelei's blog was already posted, ready and waiting for the regulars on her bulletin boards to sign on with their morning latte and read about her experience at the key party. Having Lorelei reveal something as personal as not only going to a local party, but meeting someone there, was an unusual enough event that a couple of thousand hits and some lively traffic were guaranteed. And if even a small percentage of those people went out and bought the paper to read her article, the Q of P would leave her alone. Maybe for as long as a week.

It was a good article. She might even be able to use it in her clip portfolio if she ever landed an interview at *Left Coast*.

*Left Coast.*

Josh.

Lauren's concentration shattered. Again.

The locks rattled and Vivien slipped through the door, looking a little disheveled. Lauren glanced over her shoulder and smiled.

"Hey, girl. Want a nightcap? Rory scored me some of the Chardonnay left over from the party. Not to mention two boxes of yummies from Lavender Field."

Viv smiled weakly. "No, thanks. I'm going to hurt enough in the morning as it is."

"It is morning."

"I rest my case."

"Poor baby." Lauren shut down her laptop. "How'd it go?"

Viv kicked off her high heels and reached around to unzip her dress. "I met someone." She stepped out of the little turquoise-silk number and padded into her room to hang it up.

"Did you? Your key partner? Damn, I should have waited. I could have used you for a before-and-after scenario."

"I did what you said." Viv came back wrapped in her bathrobe and sank into one of their retro kitchen chairs upholstered in yellow vinyl. "I found someone who wasn't looking for a female partner and traded my key for his lock. But it took some doing." She sighed and cocked an eye in Lauren's direction. "Life would be so much easier if you were a lesbian."

"Sweetie, you know we'd make a terrible couple. I'm hardly ever here, for starters."

"I know, I know. But my grandma likes you."

"One of these days you're going to have to tell her."

Vivien laid her flushed cheek on the cool Formica-topped tabletop. "I can't. She was born in Shandong province, as she never misses an opportunity to remind me. They don't have gay people there, apparently. She's still very traditional, and all her friends do nothing but talk about marrying off their kids and grandkids. The disgrace would kill her. Not to mention there'd be no hope of a great-grandson to make up for me being such a flop as a granddaughter."

Viv had come out in their senior year, a miserable

year during which Lauren stuck by her through a heart-breaking romance, idealistic campus activism, and her growing inability to communicate frankly with the matriarch she both adored and feared. In Lauren's view, good friends were a rare commodity. Once she gave her loyalty, it was given for good, and she and Vivien had come out on the other side of that year as women instead of girls.

"It would end your having to go to the Saturday night suppers she sets up with eligible Chinese boys from good families," Lauren pointed out gently.

"Those dropped off after I started school again," Viv said into the table. She lifted her head. "Grandma doesn't want me to be a software geek like Dad, but it's going to happen anyway. I think she's giving up on that part."

"But you came out to him last year and he was fine with it. Maybe he could do the deed."

Viv sat up and leaned her chin on one hand. "It's not Dad's problem. I have to do it, and I can't. But the alternative is waiting for her to die, and she's in way too good a shape for that. She teaches Tai Chi to old people, for God's sake."

"Seventy-two isn't old?"

"Not in her book." Vivien sighed. "Maybe I'll have some of that Chardonnay after all."

While Lauren uncorked the wine, Vivien told her about the girl she'd met and how they'd gone somewhere else for a quiet supper. Vivien took the glass and sipped gratefully. "So what about you? I saw some tall guy with a terrific butt move in on you but didn't see the end result. No pun intended."

Lauren sank onto their secondhand couch with a sigh. The wine was excellent—much better than she could usually afford. Bless Rory's heart for keeping an eye out for her.

"The end result was orgasm. And a fine example of its kind, too." The corners of her lips turned up in a smile at the memory.

"What?" Viv clutched the lapels of her robe together and looked around a little wildly. "He's not still here, is he?"

"No, no." Lauren waved her into her chair. "He's never been here." She grinned. "We never even left the restaurant."

Her roommate stared. "Tell all. And quick."

When Lauren finished the story, Vivian grabbed what was left of her glass of wine and drained it. "Do you mean to tell me—"

"Yup."

"Right there in the—"

"Yup."

"And then Maureen—"

"Oh, yeah."

"But then what—"

"All she saw was two people kissing in an empty room, and she took it as a personal triumph. Big success for the key party idea and all that."

"Do your sisters know about this?"

After a moment Lauren admitted, "No." Mikki would think it was a hoot, but Rory, though she embraced life with gusto in other ways, was cautious to a fault about relationships. Lauren wasn't sure she wanted to hear what Rory thought of a man who could literally make a woman come with a kiss.

"I tried calling her earlier, but I think I'm going to wait until things are a little further along before I say anything," she said at last.

"Speaking of a little further along… So that was it? He lights your rocket and then kisses you good-night? Where is he? Or maybe I should ask why you're here?"

Lauren had been asking herself that for the past two hours. The left side of her brain had been busy writing copy while everything else had been permeated with Josh—the scent of him, the heat, the way his hands had felt on her skin. Everything added up to one grand, orgasmic total. Lord only knew what would happen if they actually managed to make love somewhere horizontal.

Vivien was still waiting for an answer.

"I had to get this story in."

One of Viv's eyebrows rose. "And this is a reason to not go home with someone you've actually had a chance to test drive first?"

Lauren made a face at her. "Does your grandmother know you talk like this?"

"Don't try to distract me. Come on. 'Fess up."

She tried to arrange some words that would make sense and finally gave up. "I don't know. I kind of freaked and took off afterward. I mean, he was like this tidal wave of sensation and when it was over it left me feeling kind of…"

"Washed up on the beach?"

"Nice metaphor. What am I, a whale?"

"Nah. One of those little transparent things that wiggle."

"A jellyfish. Thank you so much."

"No, not a jellyfish. Those little silver fish you can never catch because they're too fast. An apt metaphor, I would say, for someone who runs away and chooses work over doing the horizontal boogie with Mr. Come As You Kiss."

"Ow." Lauren winced. "I hate when you do that."

"What, tell the truth?"

"You and Mikki. Between the two of you, I can't get away with a single thing."

"My purpose in life is to keep you honest," Viv said virtuously. "You've got to stop doing this, you know."

"Doing what?"

"Backing away when things get interesting."

Lauren was beginning to feel a little cornered, but if she showed it, Viv would pounce. "I had to work. Besides, it puts me in control. Leaves him wanting more."

"Leaves him wondering what the hell happened, you mean. What are you going to do now?"

"I'll call him, of course."

"He gave you his number? That's a step in the right direction."

"Not exactly." She'd been so dazed by what they'd done and had had such an attack of second thoughts that she'd dashed off. "I left before I got it."

"That's okay. He's probably in the book."

"I didn't get his last name, either."

Viv raised her eyebrows. "Geesh. And here I thought you were the detail girl. The one with all the sources and resources. The one who follows up her follow-ups. What happened?"

Josh had happened. Like a tsunami or something that had tossed her around and thrown her up on a strange beach, with no footprints on it to guide her.

"I was busy coming," she said airily. "Besides, he works at *Left Coast*. I know exactly where they are. How hard can it be to find him?"

MORE OFTEN THAN NOT, Josh didn't know what to do with an in-between kind of day like Saturday. As a venture capitalist, he'd scheduled them much the same as he might a regular weekday. He'd rent a boat and take a client sailing out of the Santa Cruz yacht harbor, or he'd book a conference room at an airport hotel and catch an Asia-Pacific exec between flights to negotiate funding. Sundays were reserved for family, such as it was. His mother cooked a roast beef on Sundays, with regal disregard for heat and mad cow scares alike. But Saturdays were still a loose end.

He'd come home from the party horny and unsatisfied, but with the same sense of triumph as when he'd inked a deal. Call him kinky, but making lovely Lauren come in public had been one of the high points of his life. He wanted to do it again. Well, maybe they could choose their locations better, but a repeat was definitely on the agenda.

As soon as he could find her.

He couldn't remember a single day in his life when emotion had gotten in the way of rational behavior. Getting a name and phone number would have been rational. But amid the laughter and noise of Maureen Baxter and her crowd surprising them in the private room, Lauren had taken the opportunity to disappear. And though he'd hung around for an hour afterward, trying to find her, he'd had no success.

Yes, it was clear he was rusty in the romance department. It wasn't that he hadn't had his opportunities. In fact, Elena Vargas had made it more than clear that she and her winery had no problem taking him on as a partner in both business and love.

He had thought she was "the one," and given that relationship his best, but he'd been wrong. Still she had taught him what his limits were. And when it came down to giving all you had only to have a woman as emotionally exhausting as Elena demand more time, more money, more attention, more sex, he'd realized that there had been nothing left for him. After that he'd found himself pulling back when he started to get to know someone better. He'd been briefly interested in one of the developers in a little company that he'd funded, but even though Maddie was smart and fun to be with, it seemed that Elena had sucked out of him all the desire to get close to a woman again.

Until Lauren. He hadn't felt this sense of excitement and anticipation in a long time. Maybe never.

He stretched in his chair and tilted up his coffee cup, only to find it empty. The fog that shrouded the windows of his condo told him it would be sunny later, but he didn't mind fog. It helped him focus, and he needed to do that if he planned to put together three thousand words for *Left Coast*.

He poured the last of the coffee into his mug and rinsed the carafe, dumping the old grounds into the trash. Then he padded back to his desk and the laptop that hummed happily on it.

Buying an interest in the magazine had been easy. Being one of its contributors was not. His managing editor had told him once that part of what made him successful was his voice—a little cynical, a little deadpan, like Jon Stewart on "The Daily Show." Readers ate it up, and he was proud of the stories under his byline.

This one was a little different, though, probably because it was turning out to be permeated by a certain long-legged blonde in a black skirt. Oh, he wasn't telling tales or anything. But the key party was a kind of test case for a pet theory he had about a society with what he thought of as "Social A.D.D." A society that went for short-term solutions such as speed dating and

Internet clubs instead of good, old-fashioned relationships that took a long time to develop.

*Right,* his inner cynic scoffed. *That little interlude with Lauren sure took a long time to develop.*

He still could hardly believe he'd done it. Maybe that was why he was thinking about her so much. She'd driven him into behavior that was so unlike him it was almost freeing. And the problem with things that set you free from your own constraints was that sooner or later you landed with a thud.

But he wasn't going to think about the thud. What he needed to do was to finish up this story, ship it and break out his research skills to find her.

At noon he saved the file up to the magazine's server in John Garvey's review folder. His managing editor had a blurry definition of "weekend," too, and would appreciate having a look at the copy in advance. Then he picked up the phone.

"Garvey."

"Hey, it's me. I just put my story on the server."

"That's what I like about you, McCrae. You, like me, have no life."

"I have the perfect life. And it just got better."

"What? I heard the lottery was up to eight million."

"Nah, not that. You should have come to Clementine's last night."

"Oh, right. A meat market by any other name is still a meat market."

"It isn't a meat market. It was a charity function with benefits."

"And you got some, from the sound of it. I heard they were giving away some nifty prizes. Maureen hit me up for a year's subscription as one of them."

"We got theater tickets."

" 'We'? This is not a pronoun I usually hear you use. Wasn't there some kind of goofy matchmaking thing going on?"

"It was a key party. My key unlocked the lock of the most beautiful girl you ever saw."

"So why are you uploading articles and calling me? Why aren't you spending this fine foggy morning with this girl?"

It would sound pretty lame if he said he'd lost his head and lost her.

"I lost my head and lost her."

John was silent. "Lost her like she had a boyfriend already or lost her like she dumped you on your head and left?"

"Neither. I think she got cold feet. But I'm hoping you'll call Maureen and get the guest list out of her. Lauren's a freelance reporter. That should narrow down the possibilities."

"I'll say you lost your head. Jeez, Josh, getting the girl's name and number is like Dating 101."

"Yeah. So I was in detention the day they had that class. Are you going to help me out or not?"

"Of course I'll help you. I needed to do a good deed today anyway. Call you back in ten minutes."

Josh hung up and gazed out at the view. The fog was lifting. He'd get the number. And then he was going to see if lovely Lauren wanted to have a repeat of last night.

At a party just for two.

*From Lorelei's blog*

Do you believe in love at first sight (LAFS)? I don't, either. If you go for the romantic theory, two people can meet at, say, a key party, feel an instant connection, and somehow know that they fit together as well as his key fits into her lock. But if you're not a romantic, you laugh at LAFS. Love, you say, is a series of chemical connections and neural synapses and is built up over time, so it's pretty much impossible for LAFS to be real.

Sure, Man sees Woman and says, "Ugh. Must have sex." Woman sees Man and says, "Hmm. Lots of tools and good cave. Make strong children. Possibilities there." But LAFS? Uh-uh. Not gonna happen. Feel free to disagree with me.

Lorelei

# 4

"OKAY, SO IT ISN'T LOVE." Lauren poured herself another glass of orange juice and offered the ceramic jug to her foster mother, Emma Constable, who smiled and shook her head. "But damn, the guy gave me an orgasm with our first kiss. I have to follow up."

Michaela and Aurora exchanged amused glances. Contrary to what Lauren had expected, Rory made no wry comments about her instant lust with Josh. Was she too preoccupied with an unexpected attraction to her own key partner? With Rory, it was sometimes hard to tell.

"So what are you going to do?" Michaela cut a piece of their mother's amazing *tourtière* from the ceramic pie dish and dug into it. Mikki enjoyed food the way she consumed life—with enthusiasm and complete disregard for such consequences as weight gain and cholesterol. "You don't even know his last name. Honestly, girl, maybe you'd better stick with motorcycles."

"Research—the journalist's primary tool. As soon as the magazine office opens tomorrow I'm going to call and find out if he's there."

Michaela scraped pastry from her plate with the back of her fork. "I think you need a cooldown period before you go jumping into this."

"I agree." Emma drained her herb tea and got up to

put the kettle on the stove for another pot, detouring out of habit around an eight-foot macrame sculpture that had hung from the beam that divided the open kitchen from the living room as long as any of them could remember. "If it's meant to happen, it'll happen." Her sage-green linen skirt swirled around her ankles as she moved, and the tail of her long auburn braid, threaded now with strands of silver, brushed her hips. There was something very graceful about Emma Constable, as if every movement, every moment of living, were valuable and therefore should be made as beautiful as possible.

Emma made art out of living. Only one of the many, many reasons her foster kids loved her. One of the other reasons was her slightly unorthodox way of managing them. Lauren knew from experience that you hardly knew she was doing it until you found yourself doing the right thing in spite of yourself. Look how she and Michaela had turned out, after all. Now Mikki fought for other kids in the foster care system and Lauren had gone from being a silent, sullen teenager who viewed even a smile with mistrust to the most talked-about woman in San Francisco. Even if no one knew who she really was.

"If it's meant to be, no one will mind me helping it along a little," Lauren said.

"Yes, but what if things have changed in the light of day?" Rory speared a tomato in her salad and pointed it at Lauren. A drop of homemade dressing slid off it and back onto her plate. "That's the problem with giving in to a moment of passion. You always have to deal with the morning after. It's a cosmic rule." She glanced at her mother with a fond smile.

"Tea?" Emma brought the kettle to the table and

filled the teapot. The fragrance of smoked jasmine filled the air.

"No, thanks." Michaela lifted a paper cup with a lid. "I'm still working on my venti latte."

"You are so addicted to that stuff," Emma said. "And check out the nonbiodegradable packaging."

"But it tastes so go-o-o-d," Michaela sighed, and winked at Lauren.

"I'll have a refill." The strong Indonesian tea wasn't terribly high on Lauren's list of faves, but she drank it because she loved Emma and she'd do almost anything to bring a smile to her face.

"So you guys think I should back away." She brought the conversation back to ground. "Thanks a lot for your support."

"We just don't want to see you get hurt, honey," Rory said. "After all, you only just met the guy, and he didn't go out of his way to give you important details like his number. You don't know anything about him. Well, except about the orgasm part."

Lauren thought about Josh. About the sin in his eyes and the strength in his shoulders. About the sure way his fingers moved to bring her pleasure and the control in his body when they danced. About the way he smelled—clean and yet compelling. And yes, about the orgasm. She'd thought about that practically nonstop since the key party.

The fact was, she knew quite a lot about him. That was why, despite her sisters' advice, she was going to come out of the bushes tomorrow and launch a full-scale attack.

WHEN SHE WASN'T IN CLASS, Vivien worked part time as a clerk/receptionist/minion at one of the venture capital firms in Palo Alto. Three weeks into her contract she'd discovered that Benjamin, Roy and Simons Company, or BrasCo for short, had masterminded the funding for *Left Coast*. As a courtesy, the magazine always sent over an early edition of that month's issue. When Viv called as Lauren was driving back to their apartment on Monday after doing some research for an upcoming column, it was to tell Lauren she'd gotten her hands on the May edition.

"You're not going to like it," Vivien warned.

"Why not?"

"Because Vivien Li, girl detective, has solved the case of the mystery man."

"Viv, if you confuse me any more I'm going to get dizzy and miss my exit. What are you talking about?"

"I'm talking about this two-page spread under a by-line by Mr. Joshua McCrae, with a very nice picture, I might add. Speaking strictly from an aesthetic point of view."

A pickup blared at her as she swerved onto her exit ramp in the nick of time. "Josh McCrae? *The* Josh McCrae? The one that got that award last year for his interview with George Lucas?"

She needed to pull over. Fast.

"Well, your guy's name is Josh and this article happens to be about key parties, speed dating and other social disorders, so by using my highly developed skills of deduction, I would say yes, they're one and the same."

"Read it to me."

"Sweetie, I have twenty trunks and four of them are ringing. I have to go. See you at supper. I'm making *shui jao*."

"Vivien!" Lauren wailed, but the line went dead.

There was no point dashing to the nearest newsstand because the issue wouldn't be there yet. And Palo Alto was half an hour away, not to mention the fact that she couldn't very well bust in on Vivien in her professional capacity. There was nothing for it but to wait.

When Lauren was nervous, she cleaned. Cleaning was the ultimate therapy—it imposed order on chaos. Usually cleaning was like writing articles—she preferred having done it to actually doing it—but in times of crisis, cleansers and scrub brushes were what she turned to.

She didn't know what the article said, but from Vivien's tone, she'd better not expect castles in the clouds and happy-ever-afters. What had he done? Surely he wouldn't mention…no. Impossible. A decent man wouldn't air his personal laundry in public for the sake of selling copies.

Not even the famous Josh McCrae, who could take anybody's dirty laundry and sell it for more money than she made in a year.

By the time Lauren heard Viv's key in the lock at six o'clock, she'd vacuumed all the floors, dusted, cleaned the bathroom and taken out the garbage. The apartment had had order imposed on it with a vengeance and Viv's eyes widened as she put the bag of groceries on the counter.

"What brought this on?" She peered into the sink. "Wow. You even polished the icky crap-catcher thing."

"That is a drain trap. Nothing brought this on. I've already poured the last of Rory's Chardonnay to prepare myself, so give me that magazine."

"Uh-huh." Viv pulled *Left Coast* out of her briefcase with a flourish. "Don't mind me. I'll just cook."

Lauren had already found the pages—128 and 129—and yes, the formal photograph next to the byline was so damn fine there was no doubt that the author was Josh. How had she not connected the first name with the photograph as soon as he'd said where he worked? She'd been reading his articles for at least a year, probably more.

Chalk it up to lust. In person, Josh was much more touchable and yummy than he was in the black-and-white photo with the tie, and besides, his hair was at least four inches longer now.

She skimmed the lead, then the first couple of 'grafs.

Tiffany—a fake name—is a case in point. At twenty-five she has given up on meeting eligible men in the conventional ways—at work, at church, in a group of people with similar interests such as hang gliding or Victorian architecture. That takes too much time, she says. Time away from what? I wonder. "At a key party you don't sit around waiting for someone to approach you," she says, her eyes leaving mine once every minute or so to scope the field behind me with the attention of a general checking his troops before battle. "With the lock and key idea, you get straight to it."

But what if you don't like the person? Are you locked into the date for the evening? "Of course not," Tiffany assures me. "You can turn in your lock and get another one. Meanwhile, you've already met six other people who are trying you out."

I feel like a size-eleven shoe. This is not how I want to feel at a social event.

OKAY, SO THAT WASN'T SO BAD. A little negative, but not the stuff of which social nightmares were made. Lauren took a sip of wine, gave herself a moment to wonder who "Tiffany" had been, then read on.

> Lacey—again, not a real name—seemed atypical of the demographic. A professional in her late twenties or early thirties, she wasn't there to find a possible partner. A worthy cause needed support, so she'd turned out to support it. But when the opportunity presented itself, she wasn't above grabbing it—in the fullest sense of the word.
>
> Ever heard of flash fiction—the telling of a story by the shortest possible means? How about a flash relationship? In the span of about two hours the relationship progressed through all the stages—meet, attraction, commonality, courtship and sex—and was over.
>
> Is this what Social A.D.D. has brought us to? Right back to wham, bam, thank you, ma'am? I hope not—but at the same time, you have to wonder if the need for speed is worth it.

A sound that Lauren hardly recognized erupted from her own throat and Vivien turned from the counter, where she was putting dumplings in a pot of boiling water, an expression of alarm in her eyes.

"You all right?"

"Flash relationship—wham, bam—he's got some nerve! Flash this!" Lauren fired the magazine across the room, where it slapped the apartment door and fell on the floor like an exhausted bird.

Vivien held the pot's stainless-steel lid in front of her

face like a shield. "I take it there was someone you know in there?"

"You know perfectly well 'Lacey' was me. I could kill that man. Making it sound like I was the one—when it was he who made me—ooh!"

Viv lowered the lid. "So what are you going to do about it?"

"Talk to Michaela."

"Oh, there's a good strategy. She'd just tell you to feed him into a wood chipper."

"That's a damn good strategy."

"Effective in the short term, but fraught with consequences."

"Don't say that word!"

"What, *fraught?* I like it. It's so Elizabethan."

"No, *short term!*"

"*Short term* is two words. Come on. Think about this. I suppose it's too late to get them to print a retraction."

"Not gonna happen." Lauren was silent for a moment. "But I can do the next best thing."

"Which is…?"

"Get him to print an amendment. Another article, changing his tune."

"And you're going to do this how? Come on, these will be ready in a couple of minutes."

While Lauren helped Vivien slice vegetables for the stir-fry a plan took form in her mind.

When dinner was on the table, she popped a dumpling into her mouth and took a breath to speak, then chewed instead. "Man, I wish I knew how to make these things the way you do. Anyone ever tell you you'd make a fine wife someday?"

"Yeah," Viv said glumly. "My grandma. At least once

a month. But we were talking about you. So you're going to lambaste him publicly on your blog? That has possibilities."

"No, I can't do that. What if people put one and one together and figure out that Lorelei, who was going all dreamy in public, is actually Lacey the Flash Relationship? I can't let someone get the better of Lorelei. The dope, at least he could have given me a better name."

"It's not our names that define us, it's our behavior," Vivien said philosophically, selecting a few more pieces of bok choy.

"Who said that? Confucius?"

"No. Li Ming-mei. Grandma."

"She's no dummy, your grandma. But that's it. It's the behavior I'll change."

"Whose? Yours?"

Lauren shook her head. "No. His. He doesn't know I've seen the advance copy. But by the time it hits the stands next week I will guarantee you he'll be in so deep with me he'll never climb out again. And that will make him change his tune."

"What about you? Are you going to get in deep, too? Actually do the dirty deed and fall in love?"

"With a guy who would stab me in the back like that in public? Not a chance. I'm going to teach him a lesson. Lorelei is definitely going to be on the loose."

"God help us all," Vivien said.

JOSH HAD BARELY hung up the phone from yet another voicemail to Maureen Baxter when the in-house Caller ID system told him the receptionist was on line one.

"Someone to see you, luv."

The lunchtime relief went by the name of Jillian and affected an accent that was a weird mix of California and London. She also had a crush on Josh and made no bones about the fact that she'd like to jump his.

"Did they give you a name, Jillian?"

"What'll you give me if I tell you?"

"Professionalism, Jill," he reminded her with a private grimace. "Remember who you work for."

With a put-upon sigh, she said, "It's Lauren Massey."

Josh ran through the list of people he had calls out to and requests for appointments with, and came up empty. "Ask her what she wants, will you?"

She put him on hold and he got to listen to a local radio station for fifteen seconds. Then Jillian came back. "She says she's here to continue your discussion of last Friday evening."

Frowning, he keyed back a couple of days on the calendar in his PDA. Last Friday had been the charity key party at Clementine's. Where he'd met the lovely Laur—

Lauren *Massey*. So that was her last name. He deleted *Call Maureen* from his to-do list.

"Send her in, Jillian. Now."

"Yes, sir." Jillian disconnected with a little more speed and force than necessary, and he glanced around his cubicle. It didn't look too bad. He moved a stack of clips from the guest chair to the floor next to the file cabinet and straightened some books that were lying in a haphazard pile on the bookcase instead of in it.

As a principal shareholder in the magazine, he'd been offered the use of one of the corner offices, but he'd turned it down. He cared more about the respect of his co-workers than about executive perks. He'd had enough of those during his days as a venture capitalist, and the corner office, the Jag as the sign-on bonus and the corporate apartment didn't interest him anymore.

Creative respect did. No one on the staff outside of Tina Bianchi and John Garvey knew that he was more than just a journalist. Some even thought that his rating a cubicle of his own was because he was the current "it" boy at the magazine.

He let them think that.

In less than a minute, a vision floated into his cubicle doorway and he forgot about everything but Lauren.

Toes painted candy-pink peeked out from high-heeled sandals, which did marvelous things to the mile or so of smooth, tanned leg above them. A flirty, flowered dress might have stopped just short of a public indecency charge, but the high-wattage smile did not. Nor did her eyes, which promised a list of things that began with a noontime quickie and ended who knew where.

A sudden zing in his blood propelled him to his feet. "Lauren Massey."

"Josh McCrae."

"You found me faster than I could find you. Maureen Baxter must be swamped. She hasn't returned one of my calls."

"You gave me more to go on—the name of your magazine, for starters. After that, it wasn't hard." She sat gracefully in his guest chair and he went around the desk to his own, which unfortunately meant that he could no longer see the way that skirt rippled over her thighs.

"I hope I'm not disturbing you," she said.

"No more than you did Friday night."

He met her eyes and the smile he saw there told him she wasn't going to play coy or pretend she didn't understand.

"Oh, good," she purred. "Do you have plans for lunch?"

# 5

Josh held the glass door of the Thai restaurant and Lauren made sure her arm brushed his as she walked inside. This was going beautifully. It had been a long, dry time since she'd captured a man's attention so completely, the way Michaela seemed to do without even thinking about it. Men took one look at her and saw "sex." They took one look at Lauren and saw "kid sister."

But not this man.

The chemistry that seemed to cook between them hadn't lost any of its sizzle since the key party. If anything, constantly thinking about Josh had added a kind of intensity to it, the way anticipation used to make Christmas the holiday to end all holidays when she'd been very small. Before her mom had learned to love heroin more than her daughter.

Lauren brushed the ugly thought away and concentrated on Josh, because God knew he was enough to make Christmas out of any woman's ordinary day. And until Black Tuesday, when the magazine came out and she carried out the final act of her plan, she was going to enjoy every moment of it.

The restaurant had only half a dozen tables. He seated her at one by the window, bending over her just enough to let her smell that combination of clean cotton and pine that seemed to be his distinctive fragrance.

Yum.

"Any favorites?" He sat opposite her but didn't pick up his menu.

"Aren't you going to look?" She gestured at the red-leatherette folder.

He shook his head. "I eat here a lot. I have it memorized."

"So you know what's good."

"Definitely." His gaze never left hers and the heat she saw there told her he wasn't thinking about satay and silver noodles. In that gaze she saw the slow revelation of skin in candlelight, the excitement of touch and the dark frenzy of fulfillment.

This was where the old Lauren would blush, hide behind her menu and change the subject. But the new Lauren, the one who was going to teach this man a lesson he wouldn't forget in a hurry, just returned his gaze with acknowledgment and promise. His touch was already burned into her skin, his words an echo that had disturbed her dreams, and she was looking forward to more of the same.

Because, of course, there would be more of the same. In the heat of her gaze, she tried to transmit that it was only a matter of deciding whether it would be in the unisex restroom in the back of the restaurant, somewhere in the building that housed the *Left Coast* offices, or back at the apartment of one or the other.

The waitress appeared and Lauren glanced hastily at the list of lunch plates, choosing the first green curry she saw.

"So, how is the article coming?" Josh asked when their plates arrived, steaming and fragrant with basil and lemongrass.

Lauren smiled. Oh, he was going to be sorry he'd

opened *this* conversational door. "I got what I needed and wrote up most of it when I got home, while it was still fresh."

"A night owl?" The glance he flashed at her hinted that he could help her out with her nocturnal activities. The glance she returned said that might be a possibility.

"I was charged up and had a lot to say. I figured I should get it all on paper while the ideas were there. What about you?" Nothing in her voice suggested anything but innocent inquiry.

"I won't ask what had you charged up."

"I think you know."

"If anything, I would think the charge would have been dissipated. I, on the other hand, was in quite a situation. I wish you hadn't left so quickly."

"Poor man." She twinkled mischievously at him. He was fishing for the reason she'd left, but under no circumstances could she tell him that she'd been overwhelmed by the power and the suddenness of her response to him. "All charged up and nowhere to go."

"I hope you plan to rectify that. Make up for lost time, as it were."

"Maybe." She closed her eyes as the flavor of the curry detonated in her mouth. "I see why you come here so often." She opened her eyes to see him looking a little bit slack-jawed, his fork poised halfway to his mouth. "What?"

"Do you know what you look like when you do that?"

"No, what?"

He leaned in. "Head thrown back, eyes closed, total ecstasy. Take a guess."

Her body responded to the throaty sexiness of his

voice and she felt a trickle of liquid desire moisten her panties. To cool herself down enough to keep her wits about her, she reverted to humor. "Um-mm…Meg Ryan in *When Harry Met Sally?*"

His focus didn't waver one iota. "I want to see that look again. And sooner rather than later."

If she didn't put the brakes on both her willing body and this conversation, they would wind up in the restroom, and that was not part of today's plan.

"You get to the point in a hurry." She scooped up a forkful of rice drenched in curry and raised one eyebrow. "Did anybody ever tell you that a girl expects a certain amount of lead-up? Attraction is one thing, and I'm certainly not going to argue with you there."

She took a beat to admire the intensity in the way he leaned forward, how long his eyelashes were and how his eyes had darkened with interest and speculation.

"But there are other steps along the way," she went on. "Things in common, for instance. Maybe a little courtship. You don't want to flash forward to the main event too soon and spoil the anticipation."

She bit into a pink-and-white shrimp that was perfectly cooked and tender. Was he going to react?

His eyes narrowed just a fraction, enough to tell her that the words were resonating. Hopefully, he was having a bad case of déjà vu. The words of his article were imprinted on her brain and she had no problem lobbing them right back at him.

"You're absolutely right." He leaned back and his shoulders relaxed a little. He wound some delicate, transparent noodles onto his fork and toasted her with them. "Try these. They're great."

He lifted the fork and watched in fascination as her lips closed on the savory mouthful. She swallowed the noodles and licked her lower lip slowly. She was sure he didn't realize that, with his gaze locked on her mouth, he had just done the same. "Okay, one point of commonality. We like Thai food in all its wonderful forms."

He seemed to give himself a mental shake. "Two points. We're journalists. And we like dancing."

"That's three," she allowed.

"Can we have sex now?"

Lauren choked as a bite of shrimp lodged in her throat.

"God, I'm sorry." Josh got up and thumped her on the back. "Are you okay?"

"Yes." She gulped ice water. "And no. You still forgot one step."

He sat again and counted off on his fingers. "Attraction, commonality, sex. Right?"

"Wrong. You forgot courtship. The hard part in the middle."

"Oh, that isn't the hard part. Not right now."

Even with tears in her eyes from coughing, Lauren had to laugh. "You are incorrigible."

"Focused. I prefer to think of myself as focused."

"So focus on this," she suggested. "A woman likes to be courted. It doesn't have to be very long—"

"Is a couple of hours enough?"

"—but it does have to be effective."

"You mean, long-stemmed roses, chocolate, all of that?"

"Maybe not the roses, but no woman in her right mind turns down chocolate. And remember, I like truffles."

"I have definitely not forgotten."

Lauren dropped her gaze before he singed her with

the heat in his eyes, and cleaned up the last of her curried shrimp. "We're going to have to work on you, though."

"Here's a suggestion. Do you already have a date to the Black on White Ball tomorrow night?"

"The San Francisco Society of Journalists' deal?" Lauren shook her head. "I can never afford to go to those things. The membership dues put enough of a dent in my budget."

"Would you go with me? In the spirit of courtship, of course."

She fixed him with a steady look. "That would about cover it."

"Good. Anything else we should talk about?"

"Don't forget the hard part."

He gave her a long look, fraught, as Vivien would say, with consequences. "Don't worry. I won't."

LAUREN OPTED NOT TO WALK Josh back to his office. After ninety minutes in his company, the urge to slam him up against the nearest wall and put a lip lock on him was getting to be almost unmanageable. The man put out some potent pheromones.

Better to keep the initial visits short and build up a bit of resistance before moving in for the main event. Which reminded her…

Lauren flipped open her cell phone with one hand and hung on to the overhead rail of the train with the other.

"Mikki, it's me."

"Well, since only two people in the world call me that despite all the times I've told them not to, your chances were fifty percent."

"I'm fine, thanks. How are you?"

"I'm in no end of shit thanks to my dear not-ex-husband. I'm actually beginning to empathize with the praying mantis."

"See? Now you can't get mad at Rory and me when we call you Mikki Mantis. You, too, want to dismember and eat your mate." A second too late, Lauren glanced at her fellow passengers to see if anyone was listening in, but the two old ladies in front of her were deep in their own conversation.

"He's not my damn mate." Michaela sounded as if she'd take pleasure in the dismemberment part, though, and Lauren decided Viv had been right. Feeding Josh into a wood chipper would be exactly the strategy her sister would have recommended while she was in this frame of mind. "So the lawyer who did the divorce was disbarred. So what. I'm still going ahead and filing the application to have it recognized here."

"Are you sure you want to do that? Nolan might have changed since he went away. I know you have."

"Lauren, I'm not in the mood for romantic optimism right now, okay? Is there something you wanted?"

Lauren bit her lip and tried not to feel hurt. At lunch on Sunday, Mikki had told them the story behind Nolan's sudden reappearance in her life and the bombshell he'd dropped that had turned her back into a married woman when that was the last thing she wanted to be. Mikki was reeling and prickly and trying to stay sane by working long hours.

Lauren couldn't blame her for being snappy. She smiled and changed her tone from wistful to upbeat. "I need a favor."

"Sure." The sound of Michaela's clever fingers on a keyboard came over the cell phone's background hiss. "Name it."

Mikki, evidently, wanted to heal the little breach, too.

"Can I borrow your black-velvet shawl? The one with the silver embroidery on each end?"

"You have a key. Just pop over and get it. It's in the third drawer of my dresser."

"Aren't you going to be around?"

"I am taking a weekend for one at a charming B and B in the wine country," Michaela informed her with satisfaction.

"One? I thought the prizes were for two."

"Do you seriously think I would be alone with Nolan Baylor under any circumstances? He's put my life in such a tailspin that a weekend alone with the TV and someone to serve me food sounds like paradise. Not all of us have four-star chefs for roommates."

"Viv will tell you herself she learned to cook with Grandma standing over her with a stick. But I know what you mean. It does sound nice."

"So what are you up to that requires a black-velvet shawl?"

"I'm going to the Black on White Ball tomorrow night. My silk jacket is too plain and I don't have anything else dressy enough."

"Did you win the lottery? I hear the tickets are pretty steep."

"Josh is taking me." The train went under an overpass and even the background hiss blanked out. "Mikki? Are you there?"

"I'm here," came the dry reply. "Tracked him down, did you?"

"My four-star chef is also Nancy Drew in disguise. A woman of parts."

"Evidently. I hope you know what you're doing."

"Oh, I do. And it isn't what you think."

"Uh-huh. Take care of yourself."

"Have fun in Napa. And stay out of those wine cellars."

"Don't worry," Michaela assured her. "That's the least of my problems right now."

FEELING RATHER PROUD of her skill at manipulation, Lauren had arranged to meet Josh at a little bar around the corner from the hotel where the ball was to be held. There was, after all, no point in letting the man know where she lived if she was going to drop him flat on Black Tuesday, after *Left Coast* hit the newsstands. The very thought of the public humiliation that would ensue if anyone got a whiff of "Lacey's" true identity was enough to make her grit her teeth and steel herself against the undeniable physical effect the man had on her.

She had to keep on track or her plan would fizzle. It was a good plan. In fact, one of its side effects was that she could use these few days with Josh to work his connections for all they were worth. If he could use her as fodder for his article, dammit, she could use him to land a job. Maybe more than one.

Lord knew she had to get something out of this.

It was painfully obvious that sex, in her case, did not lead to a relationship. Michaela's philosophy, if you could call it that, was that sex *was* the relationship. Maybe she should take a page out of her sister's book and just enjoy it for what it was instead of insisting on some kind of emotional backing for it.

If she only got one evening of courtship, a night of mind-bending sex and a couple of workable job leads before she lowered the boom on Josh and his poisonous pen, so be it. At least it would be memorable on all counts.

The etched-glass door of the bar swung open and it happened again—that *shazam!* deep in her belly every time she saw him without warning. As he wound his way through the tables, she took a minute to enjoy the sight.

There was certainly something to be said for a man in a tux. The stark lines of the jacket brought out the planes of his face, which contrasted with the softness of his hair. Who would have thought that a careless surfer cut could look so elegant and, well, *right* on a man? Between his height and long legs and the perfect proportions of his body, he was a heartbreak waiting to happen.

For any woman but her, that is.

His lopsided smile creased one cheek. "Hi." As he leaned in, she got a whiff of clean fabric and that piney cologne he used, and then his lips touched her cheek. But where some men would leave it at a brief kiss hello, Josh's lips lingered, as if he were savoring the texture of her skin.

"You look great," he whispered. "Love the see-through skirt."

She took a breath and tried to remember who was going to be breaking whose heart while goose bumps chased each other down the side of her neck and over one shoulder.

"Only the top layer is see-through," she whispered back as he took the seat next to her. What was it about this man that made her pulse kick into double time and her skin feel as though it were a separate organ whose sole purpose was to respond to him?

"Would you like a drink first, or are you ready to go?" she asked. She'd started out promising herself she was going to exact a pleasurable revenge from this man, but it was hard to remember that when his very glance was a caress and every time he moved his hands, her blood sped up in anticipation of a touch.

"It's up to you," he said. "Personally, I can put off listening to a bunch of overpublished bores for a few minutes."

"Tina Bianchi is giving the keynote," she pointed out. "And she's never boring. In print, at least." Tina Bianchi was editor in chief of *Left Coast*, and Lauren had every intention of wangling an introduction out of Josh before the evening was over.

Commonality, courtship, coitus—and connections. Until Black Tuesday, she was determined to have them all.

"You're right there," Josh admitted. "Okay, for the sake of you and Tina, I'll cave and endure the whole program. But you owe me." The look he gave her was pure heat.

"It will be my pleasure," she promised with slow emphasis.

It was less than two blocks to the hotel and in that time he did all the proper things demanded by the rules of courtship. He held the door of the bar open for her. He took her arm once they were outside. He walked on the outside of the sidewalk.

But it was the improper things that made the short walk so memorable. The way he'd lean over to speak and his lashes would dip as he looked at her—as if she were something delectable that he could hardly wait to taste. The way his voice took on a sensual rumble and made her wonder if he talked when he made love, and if he did, what kinds of things he said.

She seemed to have a knack for choosing partners who made love in complete silence. Well, not Carl. He did a sort of murmur and gasp as he came. But anyway. She'd do all the right things—communicate openly or with a smile and a sense of humor, depending on the guy—and still, when it came right down to it, they'd clam up on her. It was disconcerting to be the only one talking—a bit like being on the cell phone and finding out you'd been disconnected back at "Hello."

Maybe she'd add that to the list, too. Commonality, courtship, coitus, connections—and communication.

The lobby of the recently renovated Hotel Santa Maria lived up to its publicity brochures. The heels of Lauren's only pair of Ferragamo slingbacks clicked on a vast marble floor that was studded with curving oases of Persian carpet in jewel colors. A flower arrangement at least as tall as she was and about five times as wide sat on a marble table in the middle, with crouching lions forming the pedestals beneath it. From behind a pair of double doors at the far end, they could hear someone welcoming the San Francisco Society of Journalists. Josh produced two glossy, black-and-white tickets to the attendant at the door.

"Table seventy-five," the woman whispered. "You're just in time. The salads are coming out and the speeches are just starting."

"Perfect." Josh offered Lauren his arm and they walked into the huge ballroom together.

At what point in a relationship does trust kick in? At the first meeting, you pretty much expect a certain level…you trust him not to spill his drink on you. You trust him to pay for dinner. You trust him to kiss you good-night and to make a play for more. Well, okay, that part is less about trust than it is about inevitability.

But what about after the first meeting is over? What about when you're seeing each other regularly and you're giving serious consideration to e-mailing a digital picture of him to your mom? How much can you trust a guy not to talk about the night before the morning after, in the gym? And can he trust you not to talk about his vital stats with your girlfriends?

Do men have a good reason to fear a group of laughing women?

Lorelei

# 6

JOSH KNEW EVERYONE at Table 75. "This is Lauren Massey," he told the group, slipping an arm around her waist. "Lauren, the suit is John Garvey from editorial at *Left Coast*. This is Jeannette van Tasle from marketing, Paco Perez and Joanie Lam from the Web group and—" he paused, as if he'd just noticed the girl with the hennaed hair and the eyebrow ring "—Jillian MacPherson, our relief receptionist."

Lauren nodded at each person in turn and gave John Garvey a dazzling smile. If there were networking gods in the universe, they had just decided to make her day. Now if she could just keep her mind on that instead of the delicious distraction pulling out a chair for her, she'd be all set.

Nobody here knew she wrote for *Inside Out*. She had to remember that. She never came to these gigs because they were too expensive, so she wasn't sure if *Inside Out* ever sent anyone. It wasn't likely they'd show and inadvertently expose her, anyway. Black-on-white affairs, to her editors, meant a mixed-race relationship, and that was not news. That was just normal life. Association dinners were not news, either, and therefore the expense wasn't justified.

"So, Josh, why have you been keeping Lauren under wraps?" John Garvey wanted to know as he handed his salad plate to the waiter and accepted a vol-au-vent in mushroom sauce.

"Under wraps?" Josh cut up his vol-au-vent and inspected the contents. "Does anybody ever wonder what's in these things?"

"It's beef, luv," the girl with the nose ring said. Jillian, that was her name. "Beef Wellington."

"We're just not used to seeing you with anyone," Garvey persisted.

Since Josh didn't seem inclined to answer, and someone had to fill the conversational gap, Lauren said, "We met at the Baxter House benefit last week."

"Is that the home for girls?" Jillian asked. "A halfway house or something?"

"A transitional home," Lauren said quietly. "Sometimes young women are too old for the foster care system but too young to live on their own. The transitional home teaches them independence while it gives them a secure base. It's not permanent. When the girls are ready, they get apartments and jobs and all that adult stuff."

"You know quite a lot about it," Jillian observed. Lauren was pretty good with accents, but she couldn't place this one. London? Sydney? It was hard to tell.

"She's a journalist," Josh said. "Are you sure this is beef?"

"This is a five-star hotel, Josh," Joanie reminded him. "Of course it's beef."

"Who do you write for?" Jillian asked Lauren. The ring in her eyebrow winked in the light of the candle arrangement in the center of the table.

"I'm a freelancer."

"Ah," Jillian said.

Lauren got the impression that she had just been relegated to the mud at the bottom of the journalistic pond.

"Where have you placed your stuff?" Garvey, on the other hand, looked like an alert Saint Bernard, scenting possibilities.

Lauren wished she'd popped a copy of her résumé in her beaded bag. "Oh, all over. The *Good Times,* the *Chronicle, Inside Out, Wired.* You name it."

"*Inside Out.*" Jillian rolled her eyes. "I don't know how those people stay in business."

Lauren would not look at Josh. Or John Garvey. She hoped to God she wasn't blushing. So much for trying to tell the truth without calling attention to it. Why didn't Josh say something else about his dinner? Comment on the broccoli? But then, he didn't know she worked for *Inside Out,* either, so there was no help there.

"They stay in business because their sales are good," Garvey informed his receptionist. "Plus they have a kick-ass Web site."

"The supermarket tabs should be so lucky," Jillian scoffed. "That Lorelei columnist is right up their alley. Sensational and uninformed."

Lauren fought a sudden urge to hurl her dessert fork across the table like a javelin.

"Uninformed, maybe, but funny," Joanie put in. "This whole thing on love and trust and Social A.D.D. is a kick."

"Social A.D.D. is not a kick," Josh finally said, pushing his plate away. "It's kind of scary, when you think about it."

"Key parties and speed dating are scary?" Jillian slanted a heated look at him from under purple eyelids. "Not for you, I wouldn't think."

Josh waved a hand in negation. "They point to a bigger problem. People want to connect, they want to get involved, but they don't want to commit to a relationship, a dialogue, whatever."

"Like flash mobs," Lauren said. "A message goes out, people come together in one place, do their thing or shout their word, then disperse. They want to be a part of something but they don't want to commit to anything long-term, which would be activism."

"Exactly." Josh's voice held approval and the part of her that wasn't saying "Um, yeah, I have a brain, don't look at me like that" was unfurling under it like a flower.

"Or what about e-mail?" Jillian asked. "It killed letter writing."

"No, I don't think that's the same thing," Garvey said, earning a malevolent glare from Jillian. "E-mail makes communication easier. Sure, it's shorter than letters, but it makes up for it in convenience. Josh and Lauren are talking about social phenomena." He was silent for a second. "Jeez. Maybe we need an online columnist like Lorelei to talk about this stuff. A spinoff from the magazine, only with a better attitude."

"Where people can interact with the content?" Lauren smiled. "There's another one. Bulletin boards. Hit-and-run opinions."

Garvey looked from Lauren to Josh. "Obviously you should have talked to this woman before you turned in your piece for this month's issue."

"I did talk to her." Josh smiled at Lauren, a deep, slow smile that made her fingers forget what they were doing. Her fork dropped onto her plate. "But it wasn't about social phenomena."

Jillian rolled her eyes. "Spare us the gory details, Josh. You don't want to embarrass the woman. So, Lauren, have you ever gone on Lorelei's boards and responded to any of her crap?"

Lauren rescued the fork from the mushroom sauce and dabbed at her mouth with her napkin. What was the girl's problem, anyway? If she were gunning for Josh, her methods could use some work. But never mind that—she needed to get them all off the topic of Lorelei. Quickly but casually.

"Once in a while," she said. "That thing where she called for the mayor to be impeached last winter was, um, interesting."

Garvey held up his hands. "Don't even get me started on that. Change the subject."

Perfect. Lauren opened her mouth to do just that— and sucked in a lungful of air as Josh's hand slid down her thigh. Her skin tingled as his fingers parted the beaded fringe on the hem of her dress and explored the taut nylon of her stocking.

"Just because you lost fifty bucks to me doesn't mean you have to get grumpy," he told John, as casually as if he hadn't just fried her ability to think. "Bygones, remember?"

"Getting back to this Web site thing," Joanie put in diplomatically. "It wouldn't be a big deal to set up a blog. Programming-wise, I mean. If it were going to get stuck anywhere, it would be in front of the board."

Beside her, Josh shifted in his chair and the fingers on her skirt tightened. Was he turned on by touching her or was something making him tense? "Do you think the board wouldn't like it?"

Joanie shrugged. "It's hard to say. Rumor has it that the owners can be stuffy about pop culture. And a blog at *Left Coast* would have to be smart. Definitely not stuffy."

"Or like Lorelei's," Jillian said, clarifying what was at the other end of the spectrum.

"Maybe not, but you have to admit she has a talent for getting people talking." John Garvey had forgotten his dinner. He was looking into space somewhere above Lauren's shoulder. "We'd want someone to do that."

Under the damask tablecloth, Josh's fingers had resumed their exploration of her fringe. He smoothed it down and then reversed, his hot palm flat on her thigh as he dragged her hem slowly upward. Caressing. Teasing.

*Just when you thought it was safe.*

This was a two-fronted attack, she thought, halfway between despair and being seriously turned on. How could she concentrate on escaping this social morass and keeping Lorelei a secret when her whole body was responding to that illicit touch? She was going to be a gibbering wreck by the time they served dessert.

Or maybe she'd just *be* dessert. They could find a dark corner somewhere in this hotel, couldn't they? A deserted staircase where she could grab him, pull his shirt out of his pants and run her hands over his abs in preparation for diving lower. Where he could explore her thighs without having to worry about catching his boss's eye. Where—

"Why don't you see if Lorelei's available? Maybe she can double-shift."

Josh's suggestion brought Lauren out of fantasyland with a jolt. She glanced up at him, but his face was completely serious despite was his invading hand was doing to her.

*Danger. Danger.* Maybe she should bring up sports.

"Nobody knows who Lorelei is," Jillian said, as if this meant Lorelei was a bottom feeder who couldn't be trusted. "People have tried to mine the site to find out, but their security is too good." She shrugged. "She's probably a reporter who couldn't make it in print. Or a man."

"That doesn't say much for men." Paco seemed to be the strong silent type, but this was too much even for him.

"Well, you know what I mean." Jillian smiled at Paco, then glanced at Josh to see his reaction.

Where did she learn her methods? Lauren wondered. Junior high? She grabbed Josh's hand under the cloth, but he only imprisoned her fingers in his and stroked her palm with his thumb.

In. Out. In. Out.

The waiter served thin slices of cheesecake drizzled in raspberry sauce. Lauren raised her fork and tried to control the way it shook while she tasted her dessert.

*Get a grip. Think about the food.* Not bad. Not as good as the one Rory had made for brunch a couple of Sundays ago, but not bad.

"Here," Josh said. With one finger, he brushed a bit of frothy filling from the corner of her lip and licked it off with a single stroke of his tongue.

Lauren forgot to breathe. What had happened to her plan? She was supposed to be seducing him, wasn't she? But instead she was falling into those warm brown eyes. Her thighs had parted under her beaded fringe in invitation, and a rush went over her skin, making it feel hot and tight.

John Garvey cleared his throat. "Look," he said brightly. "Here comes Tina Bianchi."

Oh, God.

She'd just lost focus and embarrassed herself in front of the man who had the power to offer her a job. Lauren resisted the urge to jump up and run from the ballroom. After another brilliant smile in Garvey's direction, Lauren fixed her gaze on the keynote speaker as if the woman held the secret to eternal happiness.

ON A NORMAL DAY, Josh liked Tina Bianchi. She was smart, easy to work with and dedicated to the success of the magazine. She was one of the few people who knew about his stake in the enterprise, and she never cast it up to him whenever people wrote letters to the editor congratulating him on his articles—or complaining about them.

But tonight Tina was long-winded and a pain in the butt. When she finally wound up the keynote speech and the band came out, he felt like leaping to his feet and applauding.

But he didn't.

Instead, as soon as the band hit the first few notes of a cover of Clapton's "Layla," he grabbed Lauren's hand.

"Dance with me."

She opened her mouth to say something. He hoped it was a yes, because by the time she closed it again, they were out on the floor and she was in his arms.

"Hope you don't mind." He swung her out and then back. "John and the others are all right, but five more minutes of Jillian is going to make me start screaming."

"I'll tell you what's screaming." Her voice was a throaty purr. "You should be arrested for public indecency. How am I supposed to network when you touch me like that?"

"I thought women were good at multitasking."

"Even the most skilled have their limits, and I'm redlining." Lauren smiled up at him as their feet moved in time to the beat. "Don't be so hard on Jillian. She wants you."

"Too bad. I'm otherwise engaged."

"Are you?" The look she slanted at him was full of heat and challenge.

His arms tightened around her and, for the second time in a week, he pulled her against him, so close that he could smell the clean scent of her skin. She wore no perfume, but then, as far as he was concerned, she didn't need any.

"You know I am. For as long as you want."

"For another dance?" The music slid into something slower.

"Are you going to torture me by making me stay all night?"

She fit against him the way she had before, the rounded weight of her breasts against his chest, her thighs moving in a slow invitation against his. His breath began to speed up as his body tightened involuntarily.

"Slow down, big guy," she whispered, her lips touching his earlobe. "Jillian's getting the poisoned darts ready."

Over her shoulder, he saw that the table was nearly deserted, everyone having gotten up to dance except for Jillian, who was stirring her drink with the stem of a paper umbrella and trying to look as if it didn't matter.

He danced Lauren to the opposite side of the room, so that most of the crowd was between them. "You haven't told me how long we're staying."

"Seriously?" She leaned back against his arm, which had the effect of tilting her pelvic bones into his.

*Yeah, that's good.*

Slow down.

"You owe me for messing up my concentration at the table. Introduce me to Tina Bianchi."

That was not what he'd been expecting her to say. "Why?"

Her head tilted briefly in a shrug. "It would be helpful for me to know her. Come on. Be nice."

Josh gathered her closer. "Okay, let's make a deal. I introduce you as soon as this song is over, and then we go."

She swayed back and forth, balancing two ideas. "Hmm. Courtship versus networking. You really know how to make a girl squirm."

"I hope so." His voice dropped to a gravelly bass register and her lips parted.

"You have the greatest voice," she said, a little breathlessly.

"But do I have a deal?"

"To heck with the end of the song. Let's go talk to Tina now."

If Lauren had sex on her mind, she sure didn't show it as Josh located Tina at her table and made the introduction. She was poised and confident, and her smile had more wattage than the chandelier hanging from the plaster medallion fifteen feet above them.

"I'm so happy to meet you, Ms. Bianchi."

"Tina, please. I always like to meet Josh's friends." The older woman turned a teasing look on him. "He keeps such interesting company."

Josh stepped in before Tina could get any further and say something potentially embarrassing. "Lauren's a freelancer. She's done work for pubs as varied as the Comical—I mean, the *Chronicle*—and *Wired*."

"But not *Left Coast?*" Tina turned to Lauren and raised an eyebrow. "Why not?"

Lauren's smile faltered and reasserted itself. "I haven't found the right topic yet. At the moment I seem to be doing a lot of social pieces—trends, lifestyles, that kind of thing."

"Josh does social commentary, too," Tina pointed out. "Wait for the May issue and you'll see there's a place for that at *Left Coast*. Although his style is unique, mind you. Send in a spec proposal and tell John Garvey I asked you to."

"Thank you, Tina. I will."

Josh managed to drag her away before the two women got started on style or shoes or something. He'd seen the way Tina was eyeing Lauren's dress.

"What's the hurry?" she asked as they stopped at their table to pick up her handbag and shawl.

"We have a deal. And I saw how she was looking at those beads on your dress. Tina has a thing for vintage clothes and if you let her get started you'll be there for half an hour."

"She's got a good eye. This is a 1922 César."

"See?"

"You have a good eye, too. Most guys can't tell bead-work from balloons."

They passed the flower arrangement in the lobby and Josh handed his ticket to the valet at the door.

"That's the side benefit to doing social journalism, isn't it? You learn more than you ever wanted to about stuff you didn't know existed."

"Oh, come on. You knew the twenties existed."

"Yes, but I didn't know the bra wasn't invented until 1916." The valet pulled up in his Porsche and Josh held the door for her. He tipped the valet and slid behind the wheel. "So tell me, is everything under your 1922 César period, too?"

She shot him a slanting look, full of promise and mischief. "I guess you're going to have to find out, aren't you?"

He pressed the gas pedal to the floor.

WITH A SMILE that told her she'd better put her money where her mouth was, Josh aimed his sleek black Porsche at the freeway. Lauren gripped the leather armrest. Not because she was afraid—he was as good at driving as he was at writing and dancing—but for something solid to hold.

She'd never done this love-'em-and-leave-'em stuff before. The deliberate plan to seduce and then split. Michaela might have an impressive list of conquests and was the family expert at exit lines, but Lauren was strictly a beginner.

The longer she was with Josh, the less she wanted to leave. Face it—the man was beautiful, had a mouth and hands to die for and he could talk about vintage underwear, for God's sake!

Just being in the enclosed space of the car made her hyperaware of him. Each time he gripped the gearshift, she glanced at his long fingers and remembered how they had felt sliding over her thigh. Every move of his other hand on the wheel made the fabric of his tux whisper. And even though she was two or three feet away, the scent of his cologne intoxicated her, made her want to bury her face in the side of his neck and lick him.

When she managed to drag her mind off sex, it was to remember that he'd already introduced her to the two people who could help her career the most and she'd even received an invitation to send something in. Okay, it was a spec article, not an assignment, but that was normal for an unknown. She knew perfectly well that Tina had offered it as a favor to Josh, not because she'd ever seen Lauren Massey's byline.

So after he'd done all this for her, she was going to take him to bed and then dump him? Was she nuts?

*He trashed you in public, girl. Think about that.*

Well, it wasn't as if he'd used her real name. And he hadn't lied or embroidered the story. What he'd said was actually true.

*Oh, great. He's a nice guy because he trashed you in public and told the truth?*

She made a small sound and slid down a little in the seat.

"Sorry," Josh murmured. "I know I'm going pretty fast. Probably too fast for these damn vertical streets."

Was he? She looked around and recognized Cow Hollow, the area at the foot of Pacific Heights.

"Is my place okay? At least I know where it is."

Now there was a hint. But no way was she going to tell him where she lived and then give him his walking papers.

"Your place, absolutely," she said.

His place, as it turned out, was a condo with an eye-popping view of the bay and the glittering inverted arcs of the Golden Gate Bridge in the distance. The buildings in the complex were a mixture of concrete, steel and redwood that in the hands of a lesser architect would have been painfully ugly, but that managed to look interesting at the same time as they fit into the landscape and the rest of the neighborhood.

Oh, great. She was going to dump a man who was beautiful, interesting and financially on a planet in a different solar system.

*So what do you want with a beautiful, interesting, rich backstabber, anyway?*

Well, she could think of a few things. And she was going to get one of them shortly.

# 7

JOSH PARKED THE PORSCHE in his space under the building and a few minutes later unlocked his door and allowed her to precede him inside.

Lauren's skin prickled with awareness as he closed the door behind them. She was almost sorry when he flipped the hallway light on. Somehow, flinging yourself on a man was more doable in the dark than in the practical glow of track lighting.

She felt him close behind her as she moved into the living/dining room, which contained a massive entertainment center, a squashy couch and armchair, a really terrific Aubusson knockoff and not much else. But she wasn't in the mood for evaluating furniture. Not when her skin was tingling with the knowledge that at any moment she might feel his hands on her shoulders or back.

Then he stepped around her and headed into the kitchen. She stopped in midstep in surprise and, yes, disappointment.

"Can I get you a drink?" he asked from around the corner. Glassware clinked as he set it on the counter.

With a sigh, Lauren thought, Beautiful, intelligent, wealthy and now considerate? Just how bad could it get?

Her original plan had been to get him into bed quickly—or up against a wall, or backed into a closet—

blow his mind and leave him wanting more. Then when he called she would blow him off, leaving him in no doubt about why she'd done it.

She could blow off beautiful and rich. She'd done it before, with Luis, the guy who'd wanted to move all his relatives into their love nest. But nice? Why did Josh have to be so damned *nice?*

"Lauren? I have cheap brandy, expensive beer and a not-too-bad Merlot."

She tilted her head to look at the DVD titles behind a glass door in the entertainment center. "The Merlot would be great. Thanks."

Why was she saying this when she was supposed to be backing him up against the kitchen counter? Hadn't that been what he'd wanted at lunch the other day? Courtship was over. It was time for sex. And then she could get out of here before she started doing something really dumb, like falling for the guy.

"Here you go." Josh handed her a glass of dark, plummy wine. "I'm going to get out of this penguin suit."

"Do you want some help?" The words fell out of her mouth before she could stop them.

He quirked an eyebrow at her and grinned. "Does that mean the courtship part is definitely over?"

"Yes. Unless you really want to slip into something more comfortable." She shot him a glance that should leave him in no doubt about what she meant—and she wasn't talking about blue jeans.

"No, it's my turn to make you wait. I'll be back in a sec."

He grinned at her again, and while she was still blinking, dazzled, he strolled off down the hallway to where she presumed the bedroom was.

*Now's your chance.*

Lauren knocked back half the wine in two gulps and set the glass on the floor next to the couch, since there wasn't a coffee table. Her dress had no zippers or buttons, just a smooth, beaded neckline low enough to allow it to be pulled on—or off—over her head. Perfect for her purposes. She stepped out of her shoes. No point in wasting valuable seconds on them.

Okay, she'd given him two minutes to take off his jacket. And with a dozen buttons or so, his shirt should be off by now, too.

Silently she walked down the hall, her stockinged feet soundless on the glossy hardwood floor.

Pants by now. Maybe underwear and socks.

So that glorious hunk of man should be ready for her right about—

She pushed open the bedroom door.

TRYING TO BE A GENTLEMAN really sucked.

Josh removed the shiny black studs in the pleated shirt and managed not to drop any of them in the process. Did he have to get changed? Hell, no. What he wanted was for Lauren to be doing this. He wanted to feel her fingers opening his shirt, wanted her hands on his chest, then moving lower to unbuckle his belt. Hell, he'd let her do anything she damn well pleased.

So what was he doing in here? Slipping into something more comfortable, as she'd said, like some coy Hollywood actress?

He shook his head at himself. This whole courtship and sex thing was just a joke. He'd rushed her out of the ballroom when it was obvious she'd wanted to stay, and now he had to backtrack. Slow down. Let her set the pace. Much as he wanted to pick up where they'd left off at Clementine's, casual sex for its own sake left him cold. Lauren was fun, bright, ambitious and so beautiful she'd made his jaw drop when he'd walked into the bar tonight. And he had a feeling Mr. César hadn't meant his dress to look quite like *that*.

So what he needed to do was to get to know her a bit better. Find out the movies she liked. What her family was like. Do the whole courtship thing. Then maybe he could get his mind off—

Josh felt the sudden draft on his naked back and spun to face the door in the act of undoing the top button on his black trousers.

Lauren looked him up and down with lazy appreciation. "Hmm," she said. "Miscalculated by about ten seconds."

He didn't know whether to button up or to finish the job and do a slow striptease under that long-lashed hazel gaze. "Miscalculated what?" he finally said.

"How long it would take you to get undressed."

"Am I going too fast or too slow?"

Her gaze locked on his abs and the undone button. Heat prickled up his neck and across his shoulders.

"Now do you want some help?" she asked softly, giving him his answer.

Without waiting for him to get his brain and his mouth moving at the same speed, she crossed the room and looked up into his face. She slid one hand behind the placket of his pants while the other ran the zipper down its track. Josh sucked in a breath as the backs of her fingers did a slow dive down the sensitive skin of his lower belly. Every hair on his body stood to attention and his blood rushed south to do its duty while he waited for her to slide her hand lower and touch him.

Instead she unzipped his fly and pulled the pants down over his butt and down his legs.

"Are…are you sure this is what you want?" He kicked the pants aside amid the rush of arousal. She was kneeling in front of him, watching him swell and harden before her eyes as hot, dark blood stampeded to his groin and he forgot to breathe.

With a tug on his socks, she reminded him that those needed to come off, too. Still kneeling, she ran the palm of her hand up his calves, over a knee and up his thigh. His erection throbbed, tenting the front of his boxers.

"Oh, yes," she said softly. "Very sure. You have great legs…for a guy. Did you know that?"

Air huffed past his teeth. That was as much as he could manage for an answer. Did she have any idea of the torture she was inflicting on him just by kneeling in that position, fully dressed, while he stood there, heroically resisting the temptation to pull her toward him?

"Can I suggest a move to the bed?" he asked, marshaling all his resources to speak coherently.

"No."

She leaned in and his lungs quit functioning again. She licked a spot on his right thigh just below the hem of his shorts, then closed her lips on it and nibbled. His erection bobbed eagerly as more blood than he would have thought possible drained out of his head and into the part that meant business.

"Lauren—"

"Shh."

She nibbled his inner thigh and his determination to wait, to let her control the pace, snapped under that butterfly sensation. Bending, he scooped her up. "This game has rules for two. Now I get to play."

He dumped her in the middle of his bed and the duvet puffed around her to cup her body as she laughed up at him. "I wondered how long you'd last."

"It's not me that has the hair-trigger orgasm," he growled. "Though I'm pretty damn close right now."

Rolling onto the bed next to her, he touched the beads on her neckline with one finger, tracing an arabesque across one breast.

"Better take this off before we pop Mr. César's handiwork all over the room," he suggested softly. "Besides, I want to see your period underwear."

"So you think frilly combinations and garters are sexy, do you?" He could swear she was holding her breath as he ran a hand over her leg and fingered the hem of the dress, sparkling with its fringe of tiny bugle beads.

"You could wear a burlap bag and still be sexy." His hand slid up her thigh in its black stocking, taking the hem of the dress with it. She lifted up a little so that it didn't catch beneath her. His fingers registered the difference between the fine mesh of nylon and the softness of skin.

"What's this?" He'd missed out on this part under the tablecloth at the hotel. Obviously he hadn't gone far enough.

"Those are called thigh-highs." Her mouth was soft and full and close. "No garters required."

That smart mouth, forever saying things that intrigued him. Now he just wanted to kiss her into silence, or maybe just reduce her to making helpless little noises before they brought each other to orgasm.

With one movement he pulled the black dress over her head and tossed it onto the chair by the window.

He found her mouth and she welcomed him in, her lips parting and meeting his. Soft. So soft and mobile, slanting and teasing, taking him deeper. Making him want that same hot, wet welcome when he thrust into her. Which, please God, was going to be soon.

GOD, COULD THIS MAN KISS. Lauren wrapped her arms around his neck and pressed close, her hips moving unconsciously against his, silently urging him on. He released her mouth and ran a chain of kisses over her jawline and down her throat.

"Such soft skin," he murmured into her cleavage. She made a sound in her throat as he licked the slopes of her breasts, thrust up higher than normal by the push-up bra, and slid his tongue into her cleavage. "But no corset. I thought flappers were supposed to be flat-chested." His lips moved on the fragile, sensitive skin along the scalloped edge of the bra cup.

"I am," she confessed. "Or the next thing to it."

"Not even close." With one hand he unfastened the center clasp and the lacy bra sprang apart as if springloaded. "You're beautiful. Look at you."

She knew what she looked like, but it had been a long time—maybe never—since a man had made her feel this swollen, this aching, this desperate for his mouth on her.

"Please," she whispered.

"Please what?"

Her nipples felt distended with eagerness, her whole body straining upward to reach that mouth that could do such lovely things to her. She wasn't the aggressor now. She wasn't the one teaching him a lesson. Oh, no. She was desperate for him to kiss her everywhere, to fill her, to satisfy this blossoming ache deep between her legs.

"Lick me," she begged.

Obediently, but with a curve to his lips that told her he was going to take his sweet time about it, he ran his tongue along the lower curve of her breast. "Like that?"

"No, I need you—"

He circled her areola, careful not to touch it. "Like that?"

"Josh—"

"Or like this?"

Finally, after an eternity, his mouth closed on her nipple and she moaned at the pleasure of it. He suckled first one and then the other, using his tongue to flick the sensitive nerve endings and then his teeth, so gently and yet with such skill that Lauren writhed with it.

"Sensitive nipples," he whispered. "I like that more than a lot of cleavage. If I can please you, that pleases me."

Lauren spared a brief thought for Carl the programmer, who couldn't resist commenting on how he'd appreciated her push-up bra because it gave him more to look at.

Ugh. Bad thought. That and Tuesday. Right now there was only Josh and the way he could play her body like an instrument he'd studied for years.

With a shimmy of her hips, she wiggled under him and pressed her hipbones up into his. "More."

"Greedy, are we?"

She welcomed his weight, his heat. Craved the sensation of the hair on his legs gently abrading the smooth skin of her calves and thighs. She was desperate to wrap her legs around him and experience that first thrust, that initial stroke that would take him into the very depths of her body and fill her. "Yes. I want all of you. Now."

"I want all of you, too. You can leave your stockings on, but that pretty underwear has to come off."

In seconds, they'd divested each other of underwear and at last, at last, she felt his long body on hers. She ran her hands over his ribs and his back, feeling the solid strength of the muscles under her palms. Even his ass was firm and well shaped. She traced its contours happily, letting her hands do the seeing for her while she kissed him and toyed with his lips, tasting him and exploring his mouth.

His erection jutted between them, trapped between their bodies. "Lauren," he groaned, "I can't hang on much longer."

Neither could she. She needed him to fill her worse than she could remember needing anything. She needed to take this gorgeous man inside her and to hold him there as long as she could, imprint him on her cells, so that days from now she'd remember how it felt.

For those days when she wouldn't have him anymore.

"Just a sec." He rolled away and opened the drawer of the bedside table. Removing the little foil package from his hand, she rolled it on.

She loved the way her slightest touch could make his abs contract and his penis bob hungrily. She pulled him down onto the pillows. "Now, come here."

This time his kiss was a seduction, a promise of things shortly to come.

From the moment she'd first seen him, his mouth had tempted her, that full lower lip matched to a mobile upper that somehow managed to promise sinful pleasure and intelligent conversation at the same time. She trapped his lower lip between both of hers, learning its textures while her body adjusted to the weight of his. The hard planes of his chest rubbed her softer curves, the mat of hair tantalizing her sensitized nipples, making her want closer contact.

As if he sensed her need, he stroked her thigh with long fingers, rolling a little to the side so his hand could complete its journey around to the front. He cupped her curly mound and she whimpered against his lips.

"Are you ready for me?" he whispered. As he had done that first time at Clementine's, he slipped one finger between her folds. A single stroke in her soft wetness gave him the answer, and Lauren's whole body tightened in anticipation.

"Yes," she said on a long breath. "More."

"Tell me what you like."

She'd wondered if he spoke during sex. Now she had her answer. But strangely, she felt shy about telling him what pleased her. As if it would be some kind of investment in a future she knew they weren't going to have. As if it would be some secret thing he'd know about her that no one else did.

But her body was screaming for him, her breasts swollen and aching, her clit fluttering with impatience for his touch.

"Are you shy about asking?" He toyed with her curly pubic hair, one finger brushing it to produce a sensation partway between tickle and torture. "I can start the process of elimination." His grin was wolfish with pleasure at the prospect. "It could take a long time, though."

"No." She couldn't wait. She wanted to consume him like a luscious piece of chocolate, wanted that first explosion followed by a long period of savoring the pleasure. With a bit of pressure on his shoulder, she rolled him over onto his back and climbed on top of him. His erection beat insistently between her legs. Bracing herself on one elbow, she reached down and took him in one hand.

"How about we start here?"

Slowly she lowered herself on the firm head of his

penis, moistening it with the creamy fluid of her arousal, then began to stroke herself with him.

"Let me," Josh said against her throat, and she gave up control to him. His hips moved eagerly as he found a slow, smooth rhythm, the firm, cushiony head of his penis moving over her clit and producing waves of pleasure. When her breathing changed, he increased the pace just a fraction. She whimpered something unintelligible as the pleasure built—built—and broke. Lauren cried out, but still he didn't stop, just slowed, making her shudder with each precise stroke. When she would have fallen on his shoulder, gasping, he gripped her hips in both hands and lowered her fully onto himself. She moaned as he lifted up while she pushed down, giving her a pleasure of a different sort. With a long, indrawn breath, she felt him fill her utterly, assuaging the ache and somehow completing the wild ride of orgasm. His lashes half covered his eyes as he gazed up at her.

"I love that look," he said roughly. "Where your head's thrown back and your mouth looks as though you want to drink me in."

"I do want to." She made a sound like the purring of a kitten. "I'm drunk on you already. But now it's your turn."

His rhythm had been slow and firm, but when his grip on her hips became harder, his fingers digging into her flesh in a way that didn't hurt but told her his need was urgent, she increased her pace, stroking him from the inside. When they reached a pitch of urgency where her breath came as fast as each stroke, his eyes opened wide and he gasped, "Lauren—"

She took him deep into her body then, clenching her internal muscles so that he shuddered with the rhythm she imposed on him, and he said her name a second time with an additional note of surprise as he spent himself completely.

She grinned, as if she'd given him a gift when in fact he'd given it to her—the knowledge that no woman before her had been able to add that last extra fillip of pleasure to the tail end of orgasm and extend it a few seconds more.

A moment too late, she remembered. It didn't matter whether she was the only one or not. Because come Tuesday, he was never going to have that pleasure with her again. Somehow, intimately joined as they were, she wondered how she could think such a thing. Tuesday seemed eons away.

*You don't have to do it,* her conscience reminded her. *Don't be in such a hurry. Maybe you've unlocked a few possibilities, here.*

Lauren slid to one side and, sleepily, Josh gathered her against him with one arm. She fit as well there as she did when they danced.

*Maybe I should reconsider,* was her last thought before she slid into sated sleep.

# 8

JOSH WOKE in the uncharacteristically clear light of early morning and glanced automatically at the window. In spring, San Francisco was usually packed in fog like Christmas ornaments in cotton batting. But once in a while, a high-pressure ridge would come in and produce midsummer in the middle of May, and sailboats would appear as if by magic on the calm waters of the bay.

It was a great day to do something outdoors with Lauren. For once, a Saturday wasn't just an extension of the workweek. It was a prospect to be relished and enjoyed.

His arm tightened around the warm, sleeping woman next to him. What a night. First she'd awakened him, then he'd woken her. Each time she'd murmured something about having to leave, he'd distracted her with a kiss that had led to touching that had led to lovemaking and subsequent exhausted sleep.

And she hadn't left. Which made it even easier to plan something for the day.

Smiling, he left her curled up under the duvet and slipped out of bed. He pulled on a pair of jeans that were so old it was like wearing flannel pajamas with holes in the knees, and padded into the kitchen to start a pot of coffee. While it brewed, he checked his e-mail and his secret vice, "Lorelei on the Loose." She hadn't updated her blog yet today, but the boards were busy hashing over the topic of trust without her.

He had no idea who the woman was, but on the imaginary "do her or date her?" list kept by several of his buddies, Lorelei's name was definitely on the "date her" side. He could imagine sitting across a restaurant table from Lorelei and barely managing to keep up his side of the conversation, but as for having sex with the woman? The mind boggled and the testicles ran for cover.

A sound behind him made him glance over his shoulder. Lauren stood in the hallway in her vintage César, barefoot, tousled and frowning.

She looked enchanting.

"Bathroom's at the end of the hall," he said with a smile. "Coffee should be done in a minute."

"I can't stay."

"I know. You probably want to run home and change." He grinned. "It would be hard to crew a sailboat in that thing. I thought we could—"

"No, I mean I've got to go."

"If you don't like sailing we could—"

"Josh."

"—drive over to Point Reyes and walk on the beach or—"

"Josh!"

Finally he realized that her arms were crossed over her chest and she'd made no move toward him. Even her toes were curling against the hardwood as if they were trying to anchor her in place.

"What?"

"I—I have things I need to do today, so I'd better get moving." She smiled, but it was only an imitation of the inviting smile that had lit him up last night. "Hold those thoughts and I'll call you tomorrow, okay?"

"Well, okay, if you say so. No, wait." Tomorrow was dinner with his parents. That would mean cutting short their day and coming back at four o'clock to shower and change. It meant they couldn't sail and catch dinner on the pier. It meant no sunset walk on the beach. "Tomorrow isn't good for me."

"What about Monday?"

He made a regretful face. "Work. Unlike you free-lancers, some of us have to show up in the office once in a while." He was massively tempted to blow off his appointments so he could spend a few more hours talking to her, touching her…dragging her back to his bedroom and making love to her. But *Contact* had another funding cycle in the works and he couldn't miss the strategy meeting at ten o'clock. It would probably run until two at least, knocking out the greater part of the day. He glanced at the computer and the PDA in its cradle next to it. "I can reschedule some stuff and free up Tuesday. How about that?"

"Tuesday?"

From the look on her face, Tuesday might be the anniversary of a death in the family or some grim deadline she hadn't started work on yet.

"Okay, so not Tuesday." He reached for his wallet and pulled out a card, then scribbled his home and cell numbers on the back. "I want to see you again. So maybe we don't do a daytime thing, but surely we can work out coffee or dinner?"

"Dinner and a movie?" The color was coming back into her face. "Monday night?"

"Or dinner and a play. Those tickets we won aren't good until next month, but there's all kinds of good theater. *The Poison Plan*. Or *Wicked Game*, maybe, Chris

Isaak's show. Hell, if you like vintage stuff they're even doing *The Goodbye Girl* over at the—what?"

That did it. He really needed to get to know her better so he stopped putting his foot in his mouth every time he opened it. The color had drained out of her face again.

"Better stick to movies." She took his card and smoothed the edge with one finger. "I'll check the listings, and give you a call."

LAUREN SHUT the apartment door behind her and leaned on it, closing her eyes in relief.

Home. The guilt-free zone.

"You look like you robbed a bank and you're not sure you got away with it."

Lauren blinked and saw Vivien curled up on the couch, a mug of something hot cradled in her hands. Next to her was a young woman with cropped black hair and a razor-sharp pair of eyes.

She'd seen those eyes somewhere before. Recently. Really recently.

"Lauren Massey, I'd like you to meet Joanie Lam. Joanie, this is my roommate."

"Joanie Lam? Weren't you at the—"

"S.F.S.J. do last night. Yup, that was me."

Lauren glanced at Vivien. "The stolen key partner?"

Her roomie nodded. "The very same. Nice of you to not come home last night. Thanks."

"Anytime. Is there any coffee left?"

"Should be a cup still in the pot. And Joanie went out and got half a dozen cheese-and-blueberry croissants from Lavender Field."

"Oh, my God," Lauren moaned. "I love you."

"Paws off," Viv said equably.

The two of them looked like a pair of lazy cats on the couch, while Lauren felt as though someone had dragged her backward through a hedge.

In times of trial sent to test the soul, a woman could only do one thing. There were two croissants left in the box and Lauren confiscated them both. She put them on a plate, filled a mug with coffee and cream and had a look in the fridge. Aha. She washed a couple of strawberries and peeled a banana, then, clutching her booty to her chest, headed for her room.

Vivien raised an eyebrow as she passed. "Must've been a busy night. I can't believe he didn't feed you, that cheapskate."

Lauren popped a strawberry into her mouth. The sweet juice spurted onto her tongue and she made a sound of contentment that had everything to do with food and nothing to do with Josh or what a dope she was for thinking she could sleep with him and then dump him. "I left before we got around to breakfast."

"What's he like in the sack?" Joanie asked, sitting up with interest. "He never dates anyone at work and he's never brought a date to office functions." Joanie took a sip of her coffee, sparkling dark eyes still on Lauren. "Though there are plenty who'd like to help him out there, Jillian and Paco being at the front of the line."

Lauren turned a piercing look on Vivien. "How much did you say?"

Her roomie held up the hand that didn't have a mug in it, as if she were making an oath. "I see nothing. I say nothing." She lowered her hand and lifted an eyebrow. "But I ask lots. So…how is he in bed?"

Lauren bit into the second strawberry. "Is nothing sacred?"

"Not when it comes to sex."

"Viv's great," Joanie put in, as if this would help Lauren dish the details in return.

"Augh!" Lauren made as if to shield herself behind her plate of food. "T.M.I.!"

"Just trying to contribute. Now you tell."

"All right, all right. Josh is great in bed. More than great. He's a talker."

"Oo-oh." Viv's eyes were wide. "Score one for you."

"Score zero, actually. I might be seeing him Monday, but other than that, it's over."

"Why?" Joanie wanted to know. "He's great. Looks fabulous, has a sense of humor, keeps his hair clean. And a talker. What more can you ask of a guy?"

Lauren gazed at her for a moment then turned away. "It's a long story. Maybe when I get past the ending I'll give you guys a recap."

Joanie and Viv looked at each other blankly, but Lauren said no more. Instead she walked down to her bedroom with her breakfast. She needed to shower and change, and then it was time for a big dose of sisterhood. Since Michaela was holed up in a Napa Valley B and B with the TV remote, Lauren hoped that Rory was around to offer some wise advice.

"The guy is beautiful, has his own condo and he talks to you during sex?" Rory said incredulously when Lauren had poured out the whole story. "And you're going to dump him *why?*"

Lauren sighed. "You sound just like Vivien."

"Vivien, as I've told you many times, is a woman of taste and discretion. Plus she makes fabulous dumplings."

"He stabbed me in the back!" Lauren reined in a voice that was threatening to wobble. Nobody seemed to understand the magnitude of her problem. "He wrote horrible things—intimate things—about me, and on Tuesday everyone's going to see them."

"So what if they do? He used another name. Who's to know?"

"Only every person I met at that party, starting with Maureen Baxter. She caught us in flagrante, for God's sake. She's going to know it's me he was writing about."

In the background, the sounds of whatever Rory had been doing on her worktable stopped. "Sweetie, I think life with Lauren's Lies has made you a little paranoid."

"Ha, ha, very funny. For the five hundredth time, I never lie in my column. That's why people like it."

"Well, you live under this vow of secrecy so that no one finds out it's you stirring up trouble with the mayor and other people with highly trained teams of lawyers."

"I believe in free speech," Lauren said with dignity. "So does *Inside Out*."

"Uh-huh." Rory's tone was dry. "But Josh McCrae isn't allowed to?"

"Did anyone ever tell you that when your sister calls to cry on your shoulder, you're supposed to pat her back and give her your handkerchief?" Honestly. Rory never cut her any slack. And Michaela was worse. At least Rory was listening. Mikki would have probably given her two minutes of boo-hooing and then the verbal equivalent of a smack upside the head.

Which, she supposed, Rory had just done. Only with a little more tact.

"The only handkerchief I own is red silk and it goes with my Belle Watling costume," Rory said patiently, "but if you really needed it, you know I'd give it to you. I just think you're making a mountain out of a molehill. No one is going to think the person in that article is you. People are going to read it looking for themselves."

Lauren began to feel a little bit hopeful. "You think?"

"People look out for number one, especially if they go to parties with journalists. It's that old fifteen minutes of fame. Why do you think Lorelei is so popular over at city hall?"

"Is she?" None of her spies had ever told her that.

"That's what Michaela says. She thinks half the lawyers in the city attorney's office read you to read about themselves and the other half read you to scout out new business."

No kidding. She would have to drop that little tidbit into the conversation the next time the Queen of Pain called to invite her to a concept meeting. Maybe it was time to start tapping the rumor mill down at city hall.

The worktable thumped as Rory got back to work.

"You're not at the bakery, are you?" Lauren asked with a glance at the clock. Usually at 10:00 a.m. on a Saturday the three of them ate a leisurely breakfast and dished the dirt. But this weekend men had put a monkey wrench in their routine.

Men were good that way.

"No, I'm home."

"Is that bread I hear? Yum."

"Yes, but it's unofficial bread. Whomping the air out of a six-grain helps me think."

"About what? Don't tell me you have man problems, too. I'm sure Mikki would give you half her room at the B and B if you promise not to steal the remote."

"Who, me?" Rory's tone was calm, but the rhythm of the dough thumping on a surface hitched a little, then sped up. "We were talking about you. My advice is, give the guy a chance. But get over yourself first."

"Thank you, Dr. Constable."

"Anytime. Gotta get this into pans and I need two hands for that. Love you."

"Love you, too."

Lauren dropped the phone into its cradle on her bedside table and punched a pillow into shape against the headboard. Then she slumped on it, balancing the mug of coffee on her stomach.

What had she done? How could she switch gears now and give Josh a chance, when she'd gone into this just to seduce him and dump him?

She'd started something she couldn't finish—which was a switch. She'd gone into her relationships with Carl and Luis with starry eyes and an open heart, and both relationships had ended with them explaining how his particular concern of the moment needed to take priority over their plans—translation: over her—just for a little while. When she couldn't understand why the latest video game or the perennially needy brother-in-law needed days and months of their attention and time, they'd called her *selfish* and *unreasonable* and dumped her.

Maybe that was why she was so sensitive about Josh's betrayal. It was one more guy taking what she had to give and discounting it as if it were nothing because he had something more important to think about.

Maybe she could get over the public part of the humiliation. If Rory was right, nobody would know or care that she was the "Lacey" who offered nothing but a flash relationship. But the private part of the humiliation still stung. He'd taken something marvelous and new and turned it into story fodder, as if there were no feelings behind the experience. As if behind those moments with her in Clementine's he had been taking notes so he could use them later.

*Urrrrrgh.* Lauren set her mug on the nightstand with a clunk, grabbed the pillow and whumped it on the mattress. She understood with sudden clarity Rory's urge to beat on bread dough.

*That* was what she wouldn't let Josh get away with. Her sense of purpose, which had been weakening at the knees, got a shot of new life. And despite what everyone around her thought, that was why she was going to dump him on Tuesday.

*Let's see him take some notes on that.*

The inimitable Tina Turner once asked, "What's love got to do with it?" and we, my friends, are still asking. Can you have a fabulous sexual relationship without love? Sure. Can you have a fabulous love affair without sex? Sure. Just ask Lancelot and Guinevere. Would you want to? Ahhhh…probably not.

So what's better? Swear off love and go for sex? Swear off men and go for women? Swear off both and go for chocolate? Let's talk about it!

Lorelei

I got a sweater for my birthday. I really wanted a screamer or a moaner.

# 9

No Lauren to go sailing with. Or to walk on the beach with. Josh wandered around his apartment, coffee mug in hand, and tried to recapture the sparkle and sense of possibility that this particular Saturday had held an hour ago. It was too late to schedule a meeting and too late to call over to see if John Garvey was free.

Sunday was no different. He called Lauren's number at a reasonable hour in the morning and got a very cool female voice he didn't recognize.

"I'm sorry, Lauren isn't home."

"Do you know when she'll be back?"

"She took her laptop and said she was going to work."

She was a freelancer, so that meant "work" wasn't a physical place. "Where?"

"I gathered she was going to find a hot spot and work there."

Some people knew where all the hot spots for mobile communications were in San Francisco, but he wasn't one of them. He preferred the comfort of his own high-speed cable or the T1 connection at *Left Coast*.

So that got him nowhere, and he still had to face dinner with his folks. His mother was one of those people who took silence as a personal affront. As a child, she'd accused him of being sulky, but he wasn't. He just hadn't talked a whole lot, until he'd discovered writing.

Then a whole world of communication had opened up and he'd gone from contributing a poem about his gerbil to the fourth-grade class project to being editor of the high-school yearbook to choosing journalism in college.

Talking still wasn't his strong suit, but he made an effort in sheer self-defense when his mom was around. Accordingly, Sunday afternoon found him where it always did—seated at the mahogany dining table in his parents' house in Noe Valley.

"So how are things at the magazine?" His dad carved a slice of beef off the rare end of the roast and passed it to him. Josh took a pat of butter and watched it melt into the interior of his Yorkshire pudding.

"That's what the gravy's for, darling," his mother said for probably the four thousandth time in his life. Keeping track of people's likes and dislikes was not Mom's strong suit, which was why his dad had given up and gone with the flow. It could be worse. She could have been an awful cook. There were worse things to endure than a perfectly cooked roast beef every single Sunday of your life.

"It's going well, thanks, Dad." Josh swallowed a bite of pudding. "I have a piece in the issue coming out next week."

"We'll have to run out and get that one, then," his mother said.

"If you took a subscription it would come right to your door."

His mom shook her head. "At fifty dollars a year? You only have articles in a few of them. What's the point of spending money on the rest of them and having them stacked up all over the place?"

Josh glanced at the table with its patterned damask cloth and his grandmother's heavy silver, then up at the paneled walls of the dining room where a few tasteful landscapes hung. His father made no secret of the fact that he'd got where he was because of the careful—some would say frugal—use of money and wise investments. Old habits died hard, as he was reminded every time he opened the door to the hall closet in this house and at least fifty neatly folded paper grocery bags fell on his head.

His parents saved religiously, recycled conscientiously and never threw away anything that could be used again. His mother would probably pull the staples out of documents and reuse them, but that would destroy her manicure. Other people thought they were wealthy, but they themselves did not; in fact, they went the other way to the point that as a child Josh had actually worried that they were poor.

Maybe that was why he'd played his talents to the max and made his own money. Or maybe it was a trust thing with his dad, who was a nice enough guy as arrogant SOBs went, but the emotional connection that fathers and sons usually had just wasn't there.

As for actually having a conversation with his folks about anything other than possible investments, journalism or tomorrow's weather, that would only make them look at each other and change the subject. They weren't Victorian; in fact, they held rather liberal views about politics and justice. But he just couldn't imagine telling them about Lauren and asking his mom's advice about why she might be so elusive.

He could ask Lauren, though.

MONDAY MORNING his phone rang first thing—the private line he'd scribbled on the back of the card he'd given her on Saturday.

"McCrae."

"Hi, it's Lauren."

"I was just going to call you."

"You wouldn't have had much luck. I'm at Lavender Field having coffee with my sister and my mom. What's up?"

"I just wondered if we were still on for dinner and a movie tonight. You remember—we talked about it before you left on Saturday."

She was silent for a moment, during which he heard female voices murmuring in the background and the clink of forks on china.

"Just a second."

A bell tinkled and then he heard the sound of a bus passing. "Are you outside?"

"Yes. I'm not too keen on having everyone in the bakery hearing my private conversations."

"Not to mention your mom and your sister."

"Oh, they're all right. We're pretty tight. Not too many secrets there."

For a moment he wondered what it would be like to speak that freely with another human being. The closest he got was to John Garvey, but even with him there were some things you didn't want your editor to know. He didn't know whether to envy Lauren such closeness or to be glad he didn't have to deal with having people mucking around in his emotions that much.

"So what do you think?" he said. "Are we a go?"

She took a long, deep breath, the kind people take when they're about to plunge into cold water. "No, Josh. I've changed my mind about all of this. I was going to do this on Tuesday, when the magazine comes out, but now that I have you on the line, I may as well just do it." She paused. "So. Spit it out, Lauren." Another breath. "Josh, I've decided I won't be seeing you again."

It was a damn good thing he was sitting down. The back of his chair squeaked as he slumped against it. "Why not?" And what did the magazine coming out have to do with anything?

"It just doesn't feel right."

"Doesn't feel right." He looked over the walls of his cube, but no one was paying any attention. Resuming his seat, he dropped his voice. "It felt pretty damn right the three or four times we made love Friday night."

"Oh, don't." Her voice quivered in a way that told him he'd been right on target. "It has nothing to do with that."

Her voice held pain. But it was probably nothing to what he was feeling right now—rejection, frustration, hurt and under it all this illogical need to see her, to touch her hair and her skin, to watch those eyes light up at the sight of him. She couldn't just walk away.

Or if she did, he wasn't going to make it easy.

"Then what does it have to do with?" Garvey would be ashamed of his grammar, but he could care less. "What's the problem, Lauren? I can't deal if you're not honest. Give me that at least."

She paused, and another bus went by. "It's about flash relationships, Josh." Her voice got stronger, as if she'd rehearsed the words, practicing them until she'd got them right. "Isn't that what you wrote about me in *Left Coast?* Meet, attraction, commonality, courtship and sex, if I remember right." The words picked up speed. "All in the space of two hours. If that's all you expect from a relationship with me, then that's all you're going to get."

Josh struggled to make sense of what she was saying, but, "Where did you get an advance copy?" probably wasn't the best question to ask during a breakup speech. He grabbed the May issue on his desk and flipped to the article, which was flagged with a pink sticky note on which he'd written, *Get tearsheets*.

"Help me understand this. Where in here do I talk about you?"

"Hel-*lo*. The part about Lacey? The flash relationship? The part that everyone who was at that party is going to read and know was me?"

"That wasn't about—"

"Oh, don't give me that. I suppose I should thank you for making up a name, at least, but in the long run I think it's better that I don't see a man who would kiss and tell in such a public forum. There. I've said it."

"But I wasn't—"

"I'm not even going to ask how many people in the office know. Thanks for the introductions Friday night. They were a nice gesture, but we both know that no one at *Left Coast* is going to hire me. It's far more entertaining to read about me, isn't it?"

And on that happy note, she disconnected.

He sat, stunned, holding the phone against his ear and staring blankly at the damning paragraphs in the article, until the dial tone became so insistent that at last he hung up.

What had just happened? Did she really think he'd used her as fodder for a story? Well, he had, but not in a bad way.

*She doesn't seem to think so,* said a voice in the back of his mind. *She seems to think this is pretty bad. Bad enough to dump you on your head via cell phone in the middle of a busy street. That's bad.*

He hadn't meant it personally. It was just an anecdote.

*The minute you touch a woman, it gets personal. Remember that next time, dope.*

Next time. By God, yeah, there was going to be a next time. He was going to make sure of it. Despite what she said, Friday night had been real. It had been great. There must be something else going on with her, because he'd bet his next paycheck she was using the magazine article as an excuse.

Josh pushed the chair back so hard it rolled into the credenza behind him. He charged out of the cubicle and pushed past a startled Joanie Lam.

"I have those click-through reports you asked for," she said.

"Just drop them on my desk," he told her over his shoulder. Then he barged into John Garvey's office and practically threw the door shut behind him.

WHEN HER CELL PHONE RANG the following Thursday, Lauren's mouth was full of Mongolian beef. Since she kept that number strictly for business use, she wasn't about to let it ring through to voicemail. She grabbed a glass of water and with one disastrous gulp, sent the beef down sideways. Spluttering, she hit the talk button.

"Lauren Massey."

"Hi, Lauren, this is John Garvey from *Left Coast* magazine. We met the other week at the S.F.S.J. dinner."

Oh, God. He was probably calling to tell her how many people had written in since Tuesday to share the joke on Lacey.

"Hi, John." Cough, choke. "Nice to hear from you." Wheeze.

"Are you all right?"

Viv clapped her on the back and Lauren took a massive gulp of water. "Yes," she gasped as her trachea cleared. "I was eating lunch and it went down the wrong way."

"Should I call back?"

"Oh, no. I'm fine." Her breathing was almost back to normal. "What…what can I do for you?" Besides a guest spot on *Media Jokes of the Rich and Famous?*

"Well, I was thinking about you and did some research online. Looked up some of your archived articles at the *Chronicle* and *Wired,* talked to some people."

Who? Lauren wondered. People who recognized her as Lacey?

"I have to tell you, I was impressed. See, the thing is, you're perfect for a project we have coming up. It'd be strictly on spec, but if we use it, you'd have a foot in the door."

"What kind of a project?" she asked, getting interested in spite of herself. He hadn't brought up Lacey. That was good. Maybe this was for real.

"Have you ever heard of CyberCon?"

Lauren frowned at Viv, who raised both hands in a "What?" gesture.

"CyberCon?" What was that, some kind of fancy line of makeup? "No, I can't say I have."

"It's a trade show, full name Cyber Connection." John paused. "For the virtual reality industry. It specializes in cybersex."

"Cybersex." *Come on, Lauren. You've got to do more here than repeat everything the man says.*

Across the table, Vivien dropped her chopsticks on her plate with a clatter and stared at her.

"Yeah. You know, you strap on the headset and you're with your V.R. lover. It's a niche market, but a growing one. The technologies are pouring out of Silicon Valley, but it's still slower than the demand. This is one of the hottest shows on the west coast. What do you think?"

*I think you are unusually well informed about cyber-sex, my friend.* "Do you want me to cover it from a news perspective or do you want a social angle?"

"Well, this being *Left Coast,* it would be a social piece with a lot of high tech thrown in. I realize that's probably not your forte—"

"I can research—"

"So I've arranged for you to work with one of our veterans. As a collaboration, if you will. I think his voice is a good match for yours."

Finally, Lauren's brain caught up to what it was being required to process all at once. "Why would one of your vets be willing to work on a spec piece?"

"High tech is what he does," Garvey said easily. "But the content is going to take a little finessing. Our readership isn't conservative, but it takes someone with a special touch to cover a cybersex show in a way that appeals to the whole demographic."

"Ah," Lauren said a little flatly, then recovered. In a teasing tone, she went on, "So if I don't pull it off and Tina tosses it in the round file, it's not his fault. No harm, no foul."

Garvey laughed. "I wouldn't put it that way, but—"

The temptation to turn it down and sell the story to *Inside Out,* whose audience had no finesse and who would devour something as juicy as a cybersex show in a heartbeat, was overwhelming.

But this was *Left Coast!* The managing editor was offering her a piece that would take a lot of skill, but by God, she had skill. And a voice that was a good match for that of the other journalist. As for cybersex, well, by the time she was finished with CyberCon she'd have a piece they'd drool over. Sex and technology—what was not to like?

"Okay, I'll do it," she said. "When's the show?"

"Well, that's the problem," John said. "It opens tomorrow, Friday, at noon. I know that's short notice if you wanted to do some research in advance."

"That's okay." Barb Fraser over at *Wired* would probably send her everything the magazine had ever printed on the subject of virtual reality if she could messenger a box of Rory's sourdough rolls over there by closing time. "I can do enough by tomorrow so at least I can ask the right questions." She paused as a thought struck her. "So who's the vet I'll be working with?"

"He's one of the best. I have every confidence in the two of you. He's worked in high tech himself, which is why he—"

"John, I don't need his résumé," she said with a smile. It was kind of nice to have met this man socially first. She felt as though she could joke with him without him going all managerial on her. And he, after all, had called *her.* "I just need his name. And maybe his cell number if we're going to get together on a game plan beforehand."

"Oh, you know him," John said. "It's my best guy. Josh McCrae."

# 10

JOSH JUST HAPPENED to be looking at the door of the coffee bar when he caught a glimpse of taffy-blond hair through the window. His heart slammed into overdrive and he took a deep, calming breath.

*You got yourself into this. Now play it out.*

That meant being very cool and professional—at first. Her guard would be up; maybe she'd be angry and defensive about dumping him. He'd just stay calm and unthreatening, then, when they had settled into a comfortable journalistic partnership, he'd let whatever mojo they had start to percolate. His mistake had been allowing it to rise up to tidal wave size and overwhelm him. The woman had sensitive feelings, and he'd been so drowned in her that he hadn't seen it until too late.

All that was going to change.

They'd agreed to meet and exchange information this morning and then head over to the show when it opened at noon. A glance at his watch told him she was on time to the minute. That meant she wasn't going to start off by making him wait, but was going to treat him as professionally as he intended to treat her.

A good sign.

Lauren pushed open the door. She had a loaded briefcase slung over her shoulder by its strap and a laptop case in her hand.

He had his PDA and a steaming African blend. He hoped she didn't plan on going to the CyberCon show with all that stuff—they'd have to rent a cart.

"Can I get you a coffee?" He stood while she divested herself of her mobile office.

"I'll get it."

Ooo-kay. Independence as a defensive strategy.

He watched her go to the counter and order, and reached under the table to set the briefcase upright before someone with four coffees and a good attorney tripped over it.

"Okay," she said breezily as she set her drink on the table, "let me tell you what I've got."

"Lauren—"

"I had a friend at *Wired* send me everything they had about virtual reality, but the cybersex market has fairly specific parameters. I need to do some more research, probably over at *InformationWeek* or—"

"Lauren."

She looked up in the act of pulling a stack of tearsheets out of the briefcase. "What?"

"Will you let me apologize for the *Left Coast* article?"

"Not necessary." She took a hit off her coffee, then tapped her stacks into order. "I've already moved on."

"That's good. But I can't until I hear you say you don't hold it against me."

He wanted her to hold something quite different against him, starting with those sensitive breasts and slender hips. In fact, it was damned hard to concentrate on research when she licked foam off her lower lip, leaving it gleaming with moisture. With sudden clarity, Josh realized exactly what this assignment was going to mean.

He was going to spend the next two or three days thinking constantly about sex—in the company of a woman who made him think constantly about sex.

And who had just dumped him.

*Whose bright idea was this?* the voice in the back of his brain inquired with a snicker.

Lauren raised her gaze to his. "I don't hold it against you," she said at last. "I did a few days ago, but not now." She paused and flicked another glance at him. "I figure you owe me one. You give me everything you've got on V.R. technology, help me sell this assignment and we'll be square."

"That's a deal." He'd give her everything he had, all right. "So. What are you thinking of for a theme?"

Her eyes sparkled, an expression he'd worn himself when he had a great idea for a story and all the backup was falling into place.

"Everybody writes about technology in terms of alienation. You know, people do e-mail in place of something more personal, like a visit or a phone call. They argue on blogs, not in person. But how do you explain cybersex?"

She paused and he dragged his attention off her mouth and onto the question coming out of it. "Uh, people are avoiding a connection? Or a commitment?"

She nodded and sipped her coffee. "That's like phase two. But what about phase one?"

"There's a phase one?"

Under her business-like jacket, she wore a cream-colored cotton T-shirt with a neckline that dipped low.

"My sister and I were talking about it the other day." She leaned forward and the T-shirt gaped outward just enough for him to see the curves of her cleavage and a hint of lace. Did she have any idea what she was doing to him? He reined in his galloping responses and dragged his gaze up to her face.

"Fear of rejection comes before fear of commitment," she explained, her voice animated with discovery. "You have to get over that a dozen times before you even think about committing to anyone."

Or once. Like now, for instance. He took a deep breath and kept his gaze pinned on hers. He would not think about her breasts. How soft they had felt under his hands. How sensitive her nipples were and how much she liked his tongue to tease them—

"Josh, are you listening?"

Thank God for the mental "instant replay" function. "So people go in for cybersex because their V.R. partner can't reject them?" There. That was pretty intelligent, right?

"Exactly." She sat back, much to his disappointment. "You're not going to plunk your money down for a negative experience, are you? You want something guaranteed to be positive. A cyber partner is everything you want, rejection-free."

He wished she wouldn't use the second person in this particular scenario.

"So how are you going to approach the vendors at this show?" he asked.

"I'm not sure many of them have a social scientist on staff when they're doing product development," she said dryly. "But it will be interesting to see how many zillions of ways the industry can come up with to get around rejection."

He'd settle for one. Josh watched her fingers dance over the keys of her laptop as she made notes. He remembered how those slender fingers had felt on his skin, how she'd made him respond as they'd touched his most sensitive places at thigh and groin. He closed his eyes briefly to shut out the sight as desire arrowed through his body a second time. At least he could hide behind his paper cup. He took a healthy slug of the cooling brew.

"Not only do you get around rejection," she murmured over the click of keys, "you get a payoff. You get stimulated. Orgasm is the goal, right?" She typed furiously for a few seconds. "So what you have is that the consumer forgets about the rejection part and concentrates on the payoff. Which, if you're, say, a software vendor, nets you a repeat buyer."

Despite the way she sent his body into overdrive without even trying, Josh had to smile at the way her mind worked. She was absolutely right. It would be interesting to see if any of the startups he had helped to fund were displaying products at CyberCon.

Then he sobered. He still had to get around her rejection, with the help of his plan. He just hoped to God it would work.

JOSH ACCELERATED around a corner, driving the black Porsche with careless, one-handed grace. At the end of the access driveway was the glass-and-steel edifice that formed part of the Santa Clara Convention Center, flanked by a couple of brand hotels. The trip down the peninsula had been uncharacteristically quiet, mostly because Lauren had no idea what to say to a man she'd met two weeks ago, had sex with and then dumped two days after that.

Besides, watching him drive was worth the price of a ticket in itself. He wasn't a Type-A driver— thank God—but that didn't mean he wasn't in complete control of the cushion of space around his

fabulously expensive car. If this was what writing for
*Left Coast* did for you, there was a lovely little Volvo
S60 she'd had her eye on for about a year, thank you
very much.

But mostly she just watched his hands on the wheel,
with those long artist's fingers. That light, masterful
touch. Just the way they had operated on her body.

Now there was a memory she'd prefer to erase, con-
sidering the circumstances, but then he'd do something
like flick on a turn signal or shift gears and her gaze
would lock on his hands again.

It was going to be a very long afternoon. And if she
didn't get everything she needed for the story, she was
for damn sure not inviting him along when she came
back tomorrow. A woman could only stand so much.

They showed their credentials at the press entrance
and were issued plastic-coated passes on a string.

"I hate these things." She clipped hers to the lapel of
what she called her "safari jacket," that indispensable,
go-everywhere piece of clothing that every journalist
owned in one form or another. Hers was a blazer in a
bronze material that looked like raw silk but would
probably be found, undamaged, in a landfill two centu-
ries from now. It had two concealed pockets and three
outer ones, perfect for stashing digital camera, recorder,
batteries, business cards, credit cards and a pen without looking as though you were carrying anything at all.
On her feet were comfortable but stylish flats that
guaranteed she'd still be walking when the show closed
at six o'clock. A T-shirt and a short black jersey skirt
completed the ensemble. Practical but feminine. And effective, too, from the way Josh glanced at her legs the
way she had been looking at his hands.

*You don't care if he looks at your legs. You're suck-*

*ing his brain dry of everything it knows about virtual
reality and moving on.*

A woman in a short skirt isn't looking for male attention, anyway. It's a form of expression. Of freedom.

*Uh-huh. A short skirt at a convention produced by
geeks for a primarily male audience. Who are you trying to kid?*

Good point.

*Trying to make him jealous?*

Go away.

The double doors swung open and the noise hit them
both in the face. The show had only kicked off at noon
and already the floor was packed. As she and Josh
started down the first aisle, she saw that CyberCon attracted everyone from the businessman to the woman
on the way home from the gym, the single engineer to
the unemployed salesman looking for a job. Which only
went to illustrate her theory that rejection happened to
everyone, and everyone was invested in avoiding it.

Hmm. She pulled out her notebook and wrote that
down.

"Where do we start?" she wondered out loud.

Josh pulled her to one side of the aisle, out of the
thick traffic, and opened the glossy program they'd received at the door. "Let's see. The world premiere of the
NeuraLove suit happens at two o'clock on the main
stage. Video games are aisles one and two—we're in
one right now. Animation and 3-D is aisle four—that'll
be where the heavy hitters and big investments are—
and it looks as though aisles five and six are 'other.' You
know, peripherals like plug-in sex toys, clothing, art."
He leaned in to peer at the program. "Even a psychic.
Sexual compatibility readings. She must've got off at
the wrong train station."

Lauren thought that sounded kind of interesting, given the company, but she just nodded and glanced at her watch. "It's one forty-five. I vote for the NeuraLove suit. They gave it a whole page on the program. Whatever it is, it must be huge, so we'd better go get a seat."

A number of people in the crowd had the same idea. In fact, she and Josh barely squeezed into the last pair of seats; everyone after them had to make do with singles.

Promptly at two, the sound system fired up with a techno version of Ravel's "Bolero" and a man strode onto the stage. He introduced himself to the crowd as the CEO of NeuraLove, Inc.

"The NeuraLove suit is the culmination of ten years of technology development, mated with thirty-five thousand years of human social evolution," he said, to the wild applause of the audience. "And here it is, modeled by one of our first testers, Anaya." A curtain parted to reveal a woman in what looked like a neoprene suit reclining on a couch in the middle of a set decorated as a bedroom. The suit was legless and sleeveless and resembled nothing more than a thick, one-piece bathing suit. "The NeuraLove suit is a combination of state-of-the-art wireless technology, nanotechnology, sensors and dildonics—"

"Dildonics?" Lauren repeated. She'd bet *that* wasn't in *Webster's*.

"—to produce a sexual experience so all-encompassing, so intense, that the wearer will not even be aware of the fact that he or she does not have an actual partner present. As long as you have a mouse, you can have satisfaction."

"I have to see this," Josh murmured.

Out of the ceiling descended a monitor, a wireless

keyboard and a mouse, all on a Plexiglas sheet. As the CEO manipulated the mouse and gave the suit keyboard commands, the woman stretched and curled in pleasure.

"Sensor cups attached to her nipples give the sensation of moisture and friction," he explained as the model arched her back. "Waveforms in varying lengths against the skin imitate touch with movement and pressure. And lastly, in what we call the 'pelvic girdle,' electric impulses controlled by the mouse using this image map and a sliding scale of color intensity can actually bring our model to orgasm."

Collectively the audience leaned forward as the model writhed on the couch. Lauren caught herself doing the same and glanced at Josh. In this crowd of techies, geeks and investors, did no one think it was incredibly weird to be treated to a high-tech peep show? Even though no skin showed through the suit, it didn't stop Lauren from feeling like a voyeur as the model gripped the back of the couch with one flailing hand, gasped and cried out.

Josh sighed and sank back in his seat. Lauren would have given ten years of her life to know what he was thinking. Oh, wait, there was an easy way to do that.

She glanced at his crotch.

Hmm. At least he wasn't completely getting into the spirit of the thing, though there was plenty of squirming going on in the chair on her other side.

"What did you think?" she whispered as the CEO went on to explain the nitty-gritty of his technological marvel while Anaya recovered on her couch. "Was she faking it?"

He glanced at her, his brown eyes warm with amusement and something else. Speculation, maybe? "I hope not. This crowd is a tough sell. They'd know."

"Oh, come on. This crowd is mostly male. Men hardly ever know."

"And this comes from personal experience?" The speculation in his eyes bumped up a notch. She felt a sudden increase in the heat of his arm, too, wedged against hers because the chairs were set so close together.

Josh knew all about orgasm. Knew what it took to please her. There was no way she could fake it for him—he had been too sensitive to what her body needed. "Yes," she lied.

"With me?" His voice was low, yet penetrated her very cells the same way it had affected her the first time they'd met.

"I am not having this conversation here," she said, a little stiffly.

"Fair enough." He sat back in the metal chair. "Getting back to what we were saying, faking results in front of a roomful of people who, (a) have seen your product evolve over a period of years and (b) want to buy it, would be sheer stupidity. So, no, I don't think the model was faking it."

"How many people here are legitimate buyers, though, as opposed to people getting off on a free peep show?"

He grinned down at her. "Why don't you ask them?"

She tilted her chin at such a blatant challenge. *Fine.* He may be the magazine's golden boy, the guy with the award-winning style, but she was no stranger to good, old-fashioned legwork.

After the product demo was over and the model was mobbed by people wanting to see up close and personal how her suit worked, Lauren spent about twenty minutes doing man-on-the-street interviews with techies, marketing people and run-of-the-mill sleazeballs who had gotten off right along with Anaya.

Finally she saw a cop leaning on one of the power busses off to the side of the stage and went over to him.

"Hi, I'm Lauren Massey from *Left Coast* magazine. Do you mind if I ask you a few questions?"

The cop shrugged. "Sure."

"I guess the biggest thing I want to know from your point of view is why this product demo wasn't shut down on grounds of public indecency."

He grinned. "You want to make a complaint?"

"No, I'm just curious, that's all."

"There was no actual public indecency." He jerked a thumb up at the stage. "The model was fully clothed and performed no lewd acts herself. Her hands were in full view of the audience the whole time."

"She came in public!"

"Well, that'd be pretty hard to prove in a court of law, wouldn't it?"

"If the product works as advertised, you could prove it."

"Well, to tell you the truth, there's a lot weirder things in this show than a woman lying by herself on a couch making noises."

"What do you mean?"

"Try the third and fourth aisles."

"What, the animation and 3-D?"

The cop shoved himself off the power pole and sauntered away. "Those aisles are the main reason why this show is closed to anyone under twenty-one. And why they don't serve alcohol in the entire facility."

Lauren shut off her minirecorder with a snap and walked over to where Josh was waiting for her.

"Come on," she said. "I have a feeling the real meat

of this article is yet to come." She caught his grin out
of the corner of her eye and held up a warning finger.
"And don't even think about saying it."

# *11*

AISLE THREE was only about a hundred feet away, but it took them ten minutes of pushing through the crowd to get there. She'd been smart to wear sensible shoes and her combat jacket. She wasn't so sure about the skirt—either the crowd was thick or someone had grabbed her butt when they'd stalled near the display of dildos at the end of aisle two.

At last they emerged into the land of animated sexual fantasy. They started down the aisle, but had passed no more than two booths when Josh touched her arm.

"Look at this."

Under a banner that read Sexual Role-Play For Women was a huge screen. Two women in their twenties sat at the controls in front of it. Lauren watched the screen as a 3-D—no, make that a 38DD, blond bombshell flirted with the other characters that populated what looked like a cocktail party.

"What's she trying to accomplish?" Josh asked one of the operators.

"That's a very male way of looking at it." The operator, an Asian-American woman in a red tank top that suggested to Lauren that her model could be overcompensating, grinned at Josh as if she'd known him for years. "How are you, Josh?"

Well, that explained that.

"Good to see you, Maddie."

"Here we are, after all these years." Still smiling, the woman—Maddie—glanced at Lauren, then pointed to a score counter in the lower corner of the screen. "The point of *Contact* is to increase communication among the players through speech and touch. The more points you score with each interaction, the more successful your character is."

The red in the character's dress matched Maddie's top exactly. What was up with that?

"Is sex the jackpot?" Lauren asked, watching the bombshell nibble the ear of another character. Not something she'd do at a cocktail party, but maybe gamers didn't need to worry about things like that.

"That's also a male way of thinking," Maddie informed her. "A series of actions leading to a reward is like foreplay leading to orgasm. One-directional. With this game, there is no jackpot. Only an interlocking series of encounters."

"Fascinating," Josh murmured. "Are you seeing sales?"

"Yes, which I'm sure you're glad to hear." She smiled at him. "Women game differently than men do. Some of them buy into the male-oriented, orgasmic, explosion types, but the majority like relational gaming—if they can get their hands on it."

Josh thanked her and they chatted while Lauren picked up a brochure and dictated some notes into her recorder.

"I've never thought of foreplay as one-directional," Josh said as they moved on. "And what's up with the connection between blowing up buildings and orgasm?"

She would *not* ask about his connection with Maddie, or why he should be happy her product was selling. Maybe he'd given her an endorsement in the magazine.

"Never had an explosive orgasm?" The words escaped her before she remembered that they were no longer involved.

She had to get a grip. It was bad enough that they were surrounded by images of sex and people talking about it. All she needed was to make it personal and give him the wrong idea.

Too late.

His eyes were dark and hot behind their veil of lashes. "You would know."

That was the problem. She knew how the firm muscles of his thighs trembled with the force of arousal. She knew the way air whistled through his teeth moments before he cried out in pleasure. Oh, yes, she knew.

And he saw it in her face.

"Maybe that's why movies with explosions are so popular," he mused out loud, the skunk. Couldn't he just drop it? "They build in a period of massive tension just before the bomb goes off or the car explodes. Sometimes there's even this moment of total silence before it happens, the way a man takes a breath just before he comes."

He guided her around a mid-aisle display, and a drop of sweat trickled between her breasts. "I bet that's why those movies find their audience. It hooks into something deep and primal, right? Think we can use that in our article?"

She was never going to be able to enjoy the movie *True Lies* in the same way again. "Our readers aren't in the eighteen to twenty-five age bracket," she noted, "but we could mention it."

It wasn't fair that his mere existence made her think

about sex. All he had to do was walk harmlessly down an aisle and she wanted to reach out and stroke his sleeve. Take his hand. Slide an arm around his waist and nibble on his ear the way that damned video character had done.

*Oh, this is so not happening. Think about work some more. Fast.*

"Look," she said brightly. "Design your own sex doll."

As the developer talked about how the on-screen doll could respond to touch and sound with the mouse and a voice interface, Lauren recorded him and tried to pull herself together.

Josh was perfectly cool, discussing wireframe technology and high-speed rendering as if he hadn't just made her have her own personal meltdown. How could he do it?

Well, that was obvious. He'd taken her at her word and written her off. Despite his deliberate needling about orgasm, he saw her merely as a collaborator. A newbie he was helping out as a favor to his senior editor. Nothing more.

That was good. Right?

"…so the more you talk to the doll and touch her, the more of a personality she develops?"

Lauren came back into the conversation with a conscious effort. At least her recorder was earning its pay. Josh and the developer leaned over the keyboard and the guy pointed at the very lifelike—if boobs that big could be considered lifelike—woman on the screen.

Gaahhh. More male fixations.

"No, she's more like those doggie bots that were so popular a few years ago. You'd interact with them and the more you did, the more the recognition software had to work with to make the robot respond to you."

Lauren remembered Mikki and Rory howling with laughter over how attached people had become to their little bundles of circuitry and parts.

"The Amity doll takes that idea into the realm of virtual reality," the developer went on.

"Amity? As in *Amityville Horror?*" Lauren asked, startled.

The developer's eyes filled with an expression she couldn't identify. Pity? "Amity, as in love. That's what we called the prototype and we decided it was a good name for the software, too."

"Living in amity," Lauren murmured. "I bet she never argues, does she?"

"She's programmed with thousands of responses and reactions, most of which the user controls, some he doesn't, just to keep things interesting. See, if you touch her breasts, she does this—" Amity arched her back, inviting more "—and if you touch her so that she tells you she's turned on, then your avatar here—" with his mouse, he dragged an image of an erect penis onto the screen "—can have sex with her."

He rolled the penis between Amity's legs and the speakers mounted on each side of the screen emitted a moan of pleasure.

"Interesting," Lauren managed to say.

In about ten seconds Amity's 3-D limbs convulsed in orgasm and she cooed something.

"What was that?" Josh said. "'Ben, you're so good'?"

Lauren glanced at the guy's plastic badge. Oh, God.

"Well, I interact with her a lot," Ben said a little defensively. "The more you do, the more the recognition software has to work with, right?"

"Kind of like building a relationship," Lauren said. "Input produces a reaction, which produces more input."

The look Ben turned on her told her maybe he didn't think her brain was made of popcorn after all. "Exactly."

"But do you ever wonder if people would build a relationship with Amity and neglect their other relationships?"

Oops. The look of polite contempt was back. "It's just a game," he said, as if talking to a child. Then he brightened. "You can play in a group situation, though. She can be a member of a cybervillage and interact with multiple characters."

All with penises, one presumed. Lauren snapped off the recorder and thanked Ben for the information.

"Here's our brochure," he said, handing it to her. "Check out our Web site for a free demo."

Josh guided her past a couple of booths touting sexual role play. "What do you think? Food for the article?"

"At its very best." Over the jostling of the crowd, she caught a whiff of his cologne and closed her eyes for a moment to savor it. *Never mind indulging yourself. Back to business.* "Poor Amity. She gets no foreplay, a penis appears out of thin air and she comes in ten seconds? Welcome to the world of male fantasy."

Was it her imagination, or was he fighting a smile? "I seem to remember someone else who came in ten seconds. Doesn't sound so unrealistic to me."

Did he have to bring personal stuff up again? He was supposed to help her out by being detached and professional, not make her remember what had happened in their brief but explosive past. "You're forgetting the importance of foreplay. Amity got to know Ben before his penis appeared, so she was able to respond to him."

"So getting to know the person—or the avatar, as the case may be—is part of foreplay?"

What was he getting at? Was he taking notes so he could do a better job next time? Lauren eyed him as they sidestepped a couple of Japanese engineers. "Absolutely. That's the mental part. It has to come first, before the physical part."

"How do you explain the sex-with-a-stranger fantasy?"

"I don't explain it. It's fine in fantasy or in games, but in real life it's dangerous, as any woman could tell you."

"Some women like danger. Sex and death go together in all kinds of ways. Look at television and movies."

"Sure, but it's at a distance. If I'm going to have sex with a man, I want him around a bit first. Before we go to bed."

"Back to the courtship theory."

Lauren hated it when her own theories came back to bite her in the butt. "There's a reason for courtship."

"I don't think mental foreplay is what the Victorians had in mind."

"Are you calling me Victorian?"

But he didn't answer. He left her fuming in the middle of the aisle while he greeted someone he knew selling yet another software package. The products and images stuffing the booths were beginning to run together in Lauren's mind. Just how many ways to avoid rejection could the human brain conceive? After interviewing several product developers and their customers, Lauren had had enough.

"I don't know about you, but I missed lunch," she told Josh. "We've only been here for a couple of hours and my brain is already in overload."

"Overstimulated?"

"In a completely nonsexual way," she said firmly. She would not rise to the bait. He was obviously taking pokes at her in a passive/aggressive form of revenge for being dumped.

But if he was trying to make her angry, he was failing miserably. Every word out of his mouth just made her aware all over again of the black-velvet seduction of his voice. He wasn't conscious of it; it just happened, whether he was discussing software or making cracks about overstimulation.

And it wasn't just his voice, either—the way his lips moved when he spoke teased her, mesmerized her... made her think about kissing, dammit. She'd given up looking at him like a polite person and merely suffered the effects of listening to that melted-chocolate voice as he walked beside her.

"What do you feel like eating?" he asked. "A Polish dog at that stand over there or something substantial at the hotel restaurant?"

"A sandwich would be fine. There's a coffee shop next to the gym in the basement. I ate there when I was here for a seminar in February."

The coffee shop was as crowded as the exhibit floor, but eventually they were seated at a tiny table in the back. After they'd ordered sandwiches and iced teas, Josh slouched in his chair and raised an eyebrow in her direction.

"What do you think of CyberCon as a whole?"

Did he have to sit like that? Low on his spine, one arm slung over the back of the chair, his legs carelessly fallen apart, in a pose any woman would recognize as "come and climb on me"? And the truly aggravating part was that he was probably just as unconscious of its effect as he was of the two brunettes in Donna Karan business suits who were giving him the once-over from the line at the cash register.

Who were, of course, welcome to him since she'd dumped him and didn't care. She still had her powers of observation, that was all.

"Lauren?"

Huh? Oh, right. "Well, I've been to a lot of trade shows, but nothing like this. Imagine being the marketing person for some of these little corporations."

"It's a hungry market," Josh said. "The cybersex industry practically invented online interactivity."

"It'd be a prerequisite, wouldn't it? There's only so much you can do with e-mail."

Josh laughed and pulled a brochure out of his pocket. "Did you see this?"

She leaned over. "Oh, the e-mail robots? Yes, I interviewed one of their developers while you were looking at the V.R. gloves."

"Imagine e-mailing some automated device in the Far East just to have it yell at you for not paying it enough attention." Josh shook his head.

"Apparently the users get really attached to them."

"Yeah, but if you want to get yelled at, why not date a real person? Seems to me your rejection theory isn't holding up, at least in this case."

She took the brochure and their fingers happened to brush. She controlled the urge to jerk away when a *frisson* of sensation shot through her wrist and up to her elbow.

"I think it does hold up," she replied calmly, willing her hand not to shake. "After all, if you're writing to a love bot, it's still not a real person. It's a system-generated response based on keywords and syntax. Deep down the person knows that—they just choose to deny it."

"And the more it gets to know you, the greater its vocabulary." He paused to grin at her and something inside her melted at the way his eyes crinkled and a deep dimple formed in one cheek. "Plenty of people send me e-mail, but I'm convinced only about half of them are human."

*Not fair. Not fair you exposed me in print. We really could have been something good together.*

"Spam doesn't count," she said, then glanced up in relief as their sandwiches arrived: ahi tuna salad for her and a Reuben for him.

No way could a guy be attractive while he wolfed down a sandwich, right? She'd just wait for him to get Thousand Island on his chin or something. That would give her a reason to write him off.

*You already wrote him off,* the voice in the back of her mind reminded her.

*I know. I'm collecting backup data.*

*No, you're not. You're watching him lick that Thousand Island off his lower lip.*

Lauren took a big gulp of iced tea and ate her sandwich as fast as decency allowed. Not only was he a neat eater, he was quick, too. As she wiped her fingers on her napkin, he polished off the last of his sauerkraut with gusto.

"I love those things," he told her. "When I go to New York it's the first thing I go out and look for."

"That and cheesecake," she agreed. She reached for the check, but it disappeared into his palm before she could pick it up. "Hey!" she exclaimed.

"The magazine is getting it."

"Oh." That was different. It wasn't as though they were on a date or anything where who picked up the check changed the dynamics of who would do what later.

*Or, in your case, who won't be doing what. Are you sorry you dumped him yet?*

No. Not one bit.

Josh took care of the bill while she dashed into the ladies' room, and when she came out, he was standing outside the big glass window, stopping traffic as usual.

Talking to the traffic, in fact.

Lauren thanked the waitress and came up behind the woman Josh was listening to, belatedly recognizing Maddie. Whatever they were talking about didn't take long to wrap up. Josh glanced over at her, made the one-second sign with one long finger and shook hands with Maddie. She went into the coffee shop and Josh joined Lauren.

"Where to next?" he asked.

*You will not ask.*

She lengthened her stride to match his. He had probably been arranging something for later with Maddie. That was fine. Completely fine. She certainly wasn't going on any dates with him. A woman who dreamed up cybersex role-playing games would make any man a fabulous bed partner. They were a good match for each other.

Suddenly, Lauren felt exhausted and the thought of taking on the roar of the trade show floor and one more dumb male fantasy was more than she could stand.

"I have enough material," she said, climbing the stairs beside him. "I think I'll call it a day."

"Come on, Lauren." He paused on the stairs. She stopped on the step above him and turned to see what was holding him up. "You can't call a couple of hours and a few brochures research. Not when it's *Left Coast* we're talking about."

"You've got the technical part handled, don't you?" She dropped her voice so it wouldn't echo in the stairwell, but it only had the effect of making her sound inviting.

Which she wasn't. She was just standing here on the step above him, which put her at his eye level.

Lip level.

Uh-oh.

*Get a grip.*

Grip, yeah. On all that tall, vital male standing so close she could feel the heat from his body and taste the subtle scent of his cologne in the back of her throat.

"I'm doing the, uh, social commentary part," she murmured. "Opinions don't take as much research as tech … as, um, techical…"

"Technical?" he prompted, his mouth three inches from hers.

Some magnetic force that he generated kept her from turning and bounding up those stairs like a rabbit. Some helpless need inside her made her forget how to speak. And the desire that flared between them made her sway toward him, her gaze locked on his mouth as though it were the one thing she wanted in a building stuffed with objects of desire.

"Lauren?" he breathed against her lips.

"Mmm?"

"Work?"

"Mmm?" So close. That lower lip. So sweet. Must… have…

"Work, Lauren. The article?"

"Huh?" She reared back as though a sheet of water had cascaded between them.

Cold water.

# _12_

THERE OUGHT TO BE AWARDS given out for heroics in the battle of the sexes, Josh thought as every cell in his body urged him to reach out and pull Lauren against him.

But he resisted that urge, though his arms ached with the need to hold her and he was in a semi-permanent state of arousal just from being with her in an environment that was all about fantasy and instant satisfaction.

He didn't want fantasy. But he definitely wanted the satisfaction.

She felt for the stair behind her with the heel of her shoe and stepped up on it. "Work," she repeated. "Right. Like Maddie is work?"

"Exactly." Now, that sounded like a jealous remark. She had no reason to be jealous of Maddie, but still... He kept all traces of a smile from his lips. "We only have one aisle left to go. The peripherals. Come on, it won't take long."

His tone was cheerleader light, giving them both time to back away from the magnetic attraction that seemed to spark every time they let their guard down. He wasn't going to push her. He'd already made up his mind to that. But making up his mind in his bathroom that morning was a helluva lot different than keeping it made up when she was standing right here looking as though she would die if he didn't kiss her.

If he could just keep from spoiling it by touching her, this unspoken need between the two of them might just do the job for him. She said she'd forgiven him for using her in the article. But saying something and doing something about it were two different things.

He was in the "doing" camp. And he was willing to wait until she was, too.

Instead of turning him off, her elusiveness just made him want her more. He'd tasted her mouth and felt the sweet, wet welcome of her body. But a taste wasn't enough. He wanted to talk to her more, to hear her think out loud. Wanted to see how she wrote. Wanted to make her laugh.

And yeah, okay, he wanted to make love with her for about forty-eight hours straight.

So for now, he let the mojo build and allowed her to climb the stairs ahead of him, her little flippy skirt swinging enticingly, and lectured his body on patience.

When they got to the fourth and fifth aisles of the show, the expression on her face told him that to her, *peripherals* had meant keyboards and printers. But in the cybersex industry, *peripherals* meant, well, body parts on the loose.

Lauren picked up a long, slender attachment and turned it in her hands.

"Are you familiar with cyberdildonics?" the marketing guy said in the same tone a waiter might use to tell them the daily specials.

"No," Lauren said. "But I'm with a local magazine. Do you mind if I record you while you're telling me about it?"

"Not at all." The guy grinned at her. "I'm Rob, and we here at DigitalDick are proud of our newest product, the Bomber F16. You know, like the jet with the big load."

Lauren took a breath and when she spoke, he could swear she was trying not to laugh. "And how does the Bomber work?"

Rob brought up the inevitable software interface on the monitor. "It has what we call a *cyberskin* with a substrate of electronic technology that allows an offsite user to control it. Our target market is military families. See, from his laptop in the desert, the soldier can manipulate the Bomber to bring his significant other to orgasm."

"No kidding." Lauren sounded a little blank. "A marital aid."

Josh leaned over. "There goes your rejection theory again," he murmured in her ear.

"It'll give the article some balance." She snapped the recorder off and thanked Rob for the demonstration.

With the Bomber's brochure in her pocket, they pushed past a tight crowd.

"So, what percentage of women use a vibrator?" he asked. No way was he going to give up a perfect opportunity to get her thinking good thoughts about him again.

"I have no idea."

"Oh, come on. Not everyone is part of a couple."

"You should ask the DigitalDick people. I'm sure they've done their marketing research." She wouldn't look at him, but a little flush of color on her cheekbones told him her mind might be going in the right direction.

"Too late. It'll take ten minutes to get back there, fighting our way upstream. What about you? Do you use one?"

"No," she said a little stiffly. "And I thought we agreed not to have these conversations in public."

"I'd love to have them in private. You could wear something, say, like *that*."

They were in the middle of aisle five, where things were definitely low-tech. There were displays for sexy lingerie, Goth wear, jewelry…Lauren followed his gaze to the ten-by-ten booth showcasing Trashy Togs, a lingerie line based in Hollywood.

Lauren caught his wrist and got him moving again. He dragged his attention off the filmy items on the walls of the booth and just had time to hope that she was going to keep his hand in hers, when she dropped it. She'd also dropped the subject he'd tried to bring up and was firmly back on the article.

"What a great marketing technique," she said rapidly. "If you're attending the show without your husband, all you've seen all day is how he can have sex without you. So what do you do? You buy a black lace teddy at the Frederick's booth and take it home with you."

You did if you were really insecure.

"What if you're a guy and you wind up here in the outer limits?"

"You've been visually stimulated for four hours straight with sex presented to you in every possible configuration. Sex is practically burned onto your retinas. So you pick up a little peel-away French bra for the missus and take it home to see if it'll make her breasts look like Amity's."

That last part was so unexpected that he laughed. "Not in this universe."

"My point exactly." She clicked on her recorder and murmured a few notes into it. "I am *so* done. Can we go now?"

He paused at a small booth decorated like a Moroccan coffee bar, with a beaded curtain tied back in the doorway and rugs and pillows made of exotic paisley fabrics. "I didn't think they allowed food in this part of—oh."

The sign, in a calligraphic font halfway between a grunge fadeout and a quill pen, read How Well Do You Know Your Partner? and under that, Tessa Nichols, Sensitive.

Sensitive? Was that a title, an adjective, or a warning?

"Be nice, now." Lauren followed his gaze. "She's sensitive. Want to go in?"

"No." Okay, that was a little blunt, but he was feeling pretty done himself. And disappointed. And frustrated.

*Too much stimulation and not enough gratification.*

Not enough Lauren. Not nearly enough.

*Same thing.*

"Oh, come on," she urged him.

"I thought you wanted to leave?"

"This woman is selling something that has neither processor nor pixel, requires no power and needs two humans in close proximity. I don't know what she's doing here, but I'm going in for the mental break, if nothing else."

She had a point.

A young woman in her late twenties sat at a café-style table with a couple of chairs around it. Her blond hair was rolled at the nape of her neck under a close-fitting cloche hat from the twenties, and she wore— He blinked.

Too late.

"Hey," Lauren exclaimed. "Is that a César?"

The girl smiled. "I have no idea. Take a look."

She swiveled in her chair and put a protective hand on the hat while Lauren turned back the neckline of the dress and inspected its label.

"It is! Where did you get it?"

The blonde shrugged. "I don't know. A thrift shop in Santa Rita, I think. Is César a designer?"

"A big one, from the twenties," Josh said as Lauren urged the girl to her feet and walked around her, shamelessly ogling the arabesques of beadwork. She clicked her tongue in regret, tracing a finger where some of it had pulled loose and was lost forever.

"He came over to San Francisco from Paris for about three years," Lauren explained. "Critics called it his 'Barbary Coast' period, when he created some of his best dresses."

"Wow." The girl looked impressed as Lauren took a seat in one of the chairs. "Are you into fashion?"

"No, I'm a reporter. But I love his dresses." Lauren leaned over. "This is Josh. Ask him when the bra was invented. Are you Tessa?"

"Yes, I am."

Lauren gave her a card. "I'm Lauren Massey. We're taking a break from all this insanity and your booth seemed a good place to do it. If you ever want to unload that dress, give me a call."

"You can have it right now, if you want."

"Oh, no, I didn't mean—"

Tessa tossed her hat on the table and stripped the dress off over her head, revealing a black leotard under it. "I only paid five bucks for it. Anyone who knows that much about it deserves to have it."

Lauren looked as if the Second Coming had happened right before her eyes. "Oh, my God. You can't be serious."

Tessa shrugged and readjusted the hat on her hair. "It's just a dress."

"Do you know how much you could get for this on eBay?"

"I've never used eBay."

"Never?" Josh wasn't a junkie, but John Garvey was. The owner of a 1967 Corvair had to be—it was the only way to get car parts.

"Nope. So, would you like a reading?"

Josh replied, since Lauren was looking at the heap of silk jacquard in her lap and, from the signs, trying not to hyperventilate. "What's a 'sensitive'?"

Tessa leaned over and pulled a long silk scarf out of a big tote bag behind her chair, stood and wrapped it around a pair of slender hips, sarong-style.

"There. Black is good for under things, but I like a bit of color on the outside." She sat down again. "A sensitive is just that—a person sensitive to vibes from other people."

"Do you predict the future?" Josh asked. Maybe that's how she'd gotten past the show's screening committee.

"It depends." She nodded toward a deck of Tarot cards on the table. "Sometimes those help. Sometimes I just touch a person or some of their clothes and I get a lot of information about them." She paused and looked into the distance. "Sometimes I have dreams about people." She blinked and smiled at each of them in turn. "My sister is a cop. She says I'm full of it."

"Not very good advertising, is she?" Josh smiled in return.

"She deals in facts and logic and what she calls intuition, which is just close observation of her subject."

"A lot of so-called fortune-tellers use the same methods."

Tessa grinned. "Don't tell Linn that. She'd be so insulted."

"Well, since we're here and you just gave Lauren the

clothes off your back, why don't we give it a whirl?"
Tessa was so cute and unthreatening, he was willing to
play the rube and go along with her scam. It would be
entertaining, at least. And harmless. "What do I have to
do?"

"Depends. I can do a sexual compatibility reading,
if you like. Are you sleeping together?"

Lauren's head jerked up and she stared at Tessa.
Scarlet washed into her cheeks and Josh raised his eyebrows. Wow. He hadn't seen a woman in San Francisco
blush quite like that in probably a decade.

She looked great in a blush.

They looked at each other for a confused moment.
He kept his mouth shut, giving her the opportunity to
reply.

"Not…not now," she stammered, after a couple of
uncomfortable seconds.

"We're here on business, collaborating on an article,"
Josh said to help her out and fill the little silence.

Tessa's gaze was intense and very blue as it moved
from one to the other. Then she reached for her Tarot
cards and spread the deck in a fan in front of Josh.
"Okay. No reading. We'll try something else. Choose
any three."

Just like any fairgrounds shyster. Pick a card, any
card. Mentally, Josh divided the fan into thirds and
pulled one from the left, the middle and the right.

Tessa turned them over, leaned on her elbows and
studied them. She glanced up at him, then at Lauren,
who hadn't said a word but whose face had regained its
normal color. Lauren's body language, however, plainly
said, "I'm not playing." She sat back in her chair, her
arms crossed over the plum panels of the César dress
in her lap.

"Interesting," Tessa said. "This is called the Celtic love cross, okay? So here in the Love position you've got the Ace of Wands."

"What does it mean?" Josh peered at the card, which looked like a—gee, how appropriate—phallus. In the Love position. Maybe it was a sign.

"The wands represent enterprise and risk-taking. I'm betting you're into the stock market or venture capital. Technology. Something like that."

Josh felt his skin cool, as though he were going pale. "Something like that." He forced the words out. She'd better not go into any more details in front of Lauren or he'd be the one turning red and refusing to play.

"The Ace is a new beginning of some kind, a commitment to building something larger. And in the Love position, this probably doesn't mean a startup—unless work is your first love."

Wow. This girl was good. Work certainly had been his first love—until he'd decided that his life was even emptier than his parents' and he'd taken a wild swerve and met Lauren.

Lauren. New beginnings. Phallic symbols in the Love position. Things were looking up.

"The Ace of Wands personifies an aroused Will that is totally focused on the goal." Tessa waved an arm at the show booths around them. "Plenty of arousal and focus in here, but that's not what I mean. I'm talking about how you perceive yourself in a relationship, your identity. The role you saw yourself playing may not be the one that's right for you."

Role-playing? Is that how she'd received her vendor's badge? And didn't that belong back in aisle three?

"Now, here's the Nine of Swords in the Situation position." She glanced at Lauren and Josh could swear there was concern in her eyes. "You're probably not going to like this, Lauren, but it's what the cards say. Don't shoot me, okay?"

Lauren seemed to have remembered that this woman had just given her a vintage dress, and sitting and glowering wasn't a very effective way to pay her back. "No problem," she said lightly, sitting up and looking the cards over. "Go right ahead."

"This card refers to social stuff or circumstances that could be affecting your life right now, Josh. So here's the Nine of Swords, which if you look at it, shows a woman alone in the world. See how she's sitting up in bed, grieving, afraid of her own vulnerability?"

Josh glanced at Lauren and tensed with sudden concern. Instead of a blush, her face had gone dead-white and she was staring at Tessa with an expression that mixed betrayal with fear.

He opened his mouth to ask if she was all right, but Tessa was talking to him.

"I'm betting that you've come close to abandonment or some kind of tragic loss. Or someone close to you has."

She glanced at Lauren. To Josh's horror, he saw that the hazel eyes that so captivated him were swimming with tears. As he watched, one ran down Lauren's cheek.

"How dare you," she choked. "I'm out of here. And you can keep your dress."

Lauren threw the bundle of fabric onto her chair and power-walked out of the booth, pushing her way between the patrons of aisle five as she aimed for the nearest exit like a guided missile.

Josh leaped to his feet to follow her, but Tessa grabbed his wrist with a grip that was surprisingly strong.

"Don't go yet," she said urgently. "You need to hear the rest of it."

"Are you nuts?" He tried to disengage his wrist, but she hung on. "What did you do to her?"

"It's not me. It's her life that's done it to her. She's suffered a loss, hasn't she?"

"Most foster kids have. Please let go."

"Ah. I knew it. Listen. This is going to impact your relationship. It probably already has. But you have a lot to offer her."

"She isn't taking anything from me right now except a bunch of copy about technology. I said, let go, Ms. Nichols."

"I can't. Please sit, just for thirty seconds."

Josh glanced toward the exit sign above the heads of the crowd, but Lauren was nowhere in sight. If she wasn't standing by the car when he got there he was going to have to have her paged. Or come back to Tessa Nichols and have her locate Lauren in her goddamn crystal ball.

"Thirty seconds. Make it fast."

"She needs to heal and you can help her. But you have to keep a clear head. Look at the third card. It's Temperance. And it's in the Challenges position."

"What the hell does that mean?"

"It's the solution to this. It means you can gradually phase in changes in your relationship while you let go of the old stuff. Both of you have a lot of stuff to let go of, right? You can change things, but you have to remember that healing is a process, not an event. Do it a little at a time. Remember the Ace of Wands. Focus your will and intention, but Temperance means that you keep things in balance while you move your energy from the old to the new."

It sounded like a bunch of psychobabble to him. "Are we done?"

Tessa sat back with a sigh. "Yes, we're done. That'll be twenty bucks."

He flipped out his billfold and tossed a hundred on the table. "I don't know what you could get on eBay, but a hundred in the hand has got to be worth two in the PayPal system, right?"

He scooped up the dress and shouldered his way through the crowd to the door.

Thank God they'd come in his car. Otherwise it was a damn good bet he'd be walking home.

# *13*

FROM ACROSS the parking lot, Josh saw Lauren leaning on the passenger door of the Porsche, and he let out a relieved breath. None of the angry Plan Bs racing around in his head would need to go into action, but now that he knew she was safe, he wasn't sure how to handle the ride home.

He unlocked the door and held it while she slid inside, then closed it and went around to the driver's side.

"I'm sorry about that." He fired up the engine and backed out of the slot. "I had no idea what she was going to say. It's all a bunch of bullshit anyway."

Lauren was silent for so long he concluded that she was furious with him and kept his attention on the freeway back to San Francisco.

When she did speak, just as he was pulling into the parking lot under his condo, it was so unexpected that he jumped.

"I'm not so sure what she said was bullshit," she said. "It was too damned accurate."

He opened her door and held it while she climbed out of the low-slung vehicle, then he slammed it and locked it.

"It's impossible to make statements about someone's life using a tool as random as cards," he said flatly as they headed upstairs. "And she upset the hell out of you. I should file a complaint."

"She was right."

"She's a good guesser. Lots of people have unhappiness in their pasts. You could say it about anyone." His front door stuck as he tried to open it and he gave it a shove with his shoulder. Too much moisture in the fog this spring. It made the wood swell.

Lauren sat on the couch and toed off her shoes, pulling her feet up under her. "The woman on the card lost someone, so she was afraid of the future. My dad left us when I was ten. He couldn't hack my mom being on the needle."

Josh paused in the act of taking off his jacket. Something in his chest contracted and squeezed at the suddenness and bleakness of the confession. "What was she on?"

"Smack."

"He left a ten-year-old girl with a heroin addict and walked out? What a bastard."

She shrugged, sadly. "He wanted me to go with him but I wouldn't. Little Miss Caretaker. I thought she'd love me if I stayed."

"Ten-year-olds aren't supposed to take care of their mothers."

He hung up his jacket and sat beside her on the couch.

"I learned to cook when I was seven, helping out my dad. So I figured I could do it. It worked out okay as long as she was working, but when she lost her job because she was strung out all the time, there was nothing to buy groceries with. That's when Protective Services stepped in and I went to Emma's. I was fifteen."

Josh's imagination filled in the spaces between her words, presenting him with a picture of a young girl trying to find something to eat in cupboards that were empty. His mother's Sunday roast beef, which he'd been so apt to make fun of, suddenly seemed like the ultimate in luxury and parental care.

It wasn't, but compared to the picture in his mind, he should probably change his attitude about it.

"Where are your parents now?" he asked quietly.

"My mother died soon after. Emma and Michaela—my sister—made me go to what passed for a funeral. I didn't want to, but Emma said I needed to close that circle. She has this saying that the wheel never stops turning. And she was right."

"What about your dad?"

"I don't know. He wasn't there. And I've never heard from him since."

The guy *was* a bastard.

"I still look, though." Her voice was soft with memory as she sank against his shoulder. "You know, in crowded places. He could be anywhere."

Josh slid an arm around her. "I've seen you do it. Even at the show."

"The show." Lauren shook her hair back, as if shrugging away the subject of her birth family and moving on. "Imagine working on one of those products ten hours a day. Or how about being the product manager responsible for the clitoris stimulator in the NeuraLove suit?"

He smiled at the picture she made. And at the fast change of subject.

"Your wife says, 'How did your day go, dear?' and you say, 'Well, our model didn't come because the stimulator's pulse isn't strong enough. Back to the drawing board tomorrow.'"

Her voice was getting strained, her words picking up

speed like a car going down Lombard Street without brakes. Josh tightened his arm, pulling her closer.

"Lauren. Listen, it's okay. We don't have to talk about any of this if you don't want to."

It felt good to have his arm around her. Protective. A role he didn't play very often. Josh realized in a moment of piercing clarity that this was the point at which all his relationships after Elena had foundered. When the woman revealed something personal, something that showed a weakness or a flaw, something that was going to require an emotional investment from him— that was where he usually bailed. And why? he asked himself with a sense of amazement at his own arrogance. Why shouldn't a woman show a flaw or two? Lord knew he had a pantload of them himself.

*Because that would mean you'd have to care. You'd have to get involved with their problems and life wouldn't be as clean and easy as you've made it, would it?*

Was that all he wanted out of life? Clean and easy? Had he really been such a jerk?

Tessa's advice sounded in his head. Changing roles. Change happening a little at a time. Temperance.

Lauren pulled her legs in close, as if trying to burrow into him, and buried her face in his shoulder. "Make love to me, Josh," she whispered.

What? Now? When she'd just come under attack from nasty memories from the past? When she'd been laid open by a Tarot card as easily as a card key opened a hotel room door?

"I don't think that's a good idea," he said as gently as he could. "You're not—"

"I take back what I said on Monday about not seeing you again. We can reinstate that later, but right now I really need you. Please, Josh."

The rational part of his brain registered the fact that she was using him because she needed comfort, and rejecting her now would only put another layer of pain on top of an old wound. The other side of his brain was thinking about change and then it shorted out altogether as she nuzzled the sensitive skin under his ear and nibbled on his earlobe.

His personal version of the Bomber, which had been half awake all day just being with her, came fully alive as she pressed her breasts against his arm. "You're not making it easy for me to be a gentleman," he told her, then gulped as she ran her tongue around the curves of his ear.

"Don't want a gentleman," she whispered, busy again with his earlobe. "Want a bad boy with a black Porsche and a mouth made for sin."

Oh, God. She wanted a bad boy? He'd never qualified for that in his life—but if taking advantage of her when she was at her most vulnerable was what she wanted, then he'd learn to be bad.

He'd worry about being redumped later.

IF HE DIDN'T KISS HER, she'd die.

Lauren sucked on Josh's earlobe while this primal urge to climb on him and demand satisfaction grew inside her. At least she'd retained the sense to ask him first and to clarify the dumper/dumpee situation. But after that, all bets were off.

She couldn't explain it other than to blame it on the trade show and that damn fortune-teller who had reminded her of what she'd spent years trying to forget. The only cure for it was fast, mind-altering sex and as far as she was concerned, there was only one man for that.

He changed position on the couch and pulled her into

his lap. But before she had a chance to do more than register the presence of an erection that promised to alter more than her mind, he pulled her head down and captured her mouth.

Hard. Demanding. Just the way she wanted it.

She wrapped both arms around his neck and met his kiss with one of her own, hot and slick, with nothing held back. His right arm held her securely against his chest, while his other hand smoothed the fabric of the low-necked T-shirt under her jacket in one long exploratory stroke.

She released him long enough to shrug out of the jacket, and while her arms were busy freeing themselves from the sleeves, he tugged the T-shirt out of the waistband of her skirt.

"Do you like busty women?" she asked wistfully against his lips as he slipped his hand under the fine cotton and flattened it on her ribs.

"Meaning, do I like women with breasts? Yes, indeed." His hand moved stealthily north.

She stifled a huff of laughter. "Meaning, women with big breasts. Or at least bigger than mine."

He kissed her again, a long, satisfying kiss that made her forget the question until he lifted his head and she remembered to breathe. He cupped her breast and stroked the beaded, hard nipple with his thumb through the lace of her bra.

"From now on, a busty woman will remind me of Amity, and that's not an image I want to have in my head."

This time she couldn't hold the giggle in.

"You're perfectly shaped," he said softly. Pleasure spread under his fingers, making her arch her back to meet them, encouraging more contact. "Your eyes make me think bad things at inappropriate moments. Things come out of your mouth that make me laugh when I'm thinking about what else it can do. And your legs and your peachy little ass make me think about sex all the rest of the time."

His clever fingers found the front clasp of the bra and snapped it open, freeing her flesh to be touched and stroked.

"Then you can look at busty women all you like," she said generously, gasping as those long fingers slid over her nipples.

"I'd rather look at you. Without clothes. In bed. Now."

He slid his free hand under her knees and half stood. She shrieked as she felt him lose his balance and they both tipped backward and landed in a heap on the couch.

Breathless with laughter, she said, "Better save the Rhett Butler moves for later. I'm in the mood for the direct approach."

She slid off his lap and pulled him to his feet. The short trip down the hall seemed to take forever, suffused as she was by desire and need in a heady combination that could only be satisfied by the friction of skin against skin, striking sparks of arousal.

In his bedroom, Josh stopped her as she was about to pull him onto the bed. "Here. It seems to me I owe you one from last time." He knelt in front of her and skimmed both hands up the sides of her skirt. "Aha."

With a quick twist of his fingers, he unfastened the button and ran the zipper down its short track. Her skirt plummeted down her legs, leaving her naked except for hose and panties. She couldn't resist the urge to run both hands through his hair when he looked up at her.

"What, no thigh-highs?" he teased.

Was it possible to need anyone more than she needed him at this moment? Lauren felt her breath back up in her chest and she struggled to control emotions that swung from grief to giddiness, from despair to desire, between one moment and the next.

"Panty hose for work. Thigh-highs for play," she told him, trying to match his light tone. His hair was soft and warm, alive under her fingers. A mix of dark brown and blond that told her he'd been serious about sailing last weekend. This was hair that bleached in the sun. She smoothed it out of his eyes.

He hooked his thumbs in the waistband and peeled her out of both hose and panties. "That's more like it." His voice was filled with satisfaction and she felt a shiver of anticipation tiptoe across her shoulders as his gaze centered on the curly thatch at the apex of her legs.

He leaned in and Lauren sucked in a breath as he tasted, not her swollen labia, but her inner thigh, kissing his way down her leg, then taking her ankle gently in one hand. She turned slightly and he kissed the soft skin behind her knee. The other knee received the same attention and he leisurely kissed his way back up the other leg, taking his time to lick and savor every inch. By the time he reached the spot where he'd begun, she was trembling with need.

"I love your legs," he said against the long muscles in her thigh. "Wear short skirts all the time, okay?"

"Anything you want," she whispered.

She forgot she hadn't been going to see him again. She forgot he'd written about her in a magazine. All there was room to think about was his bad boy's mouth and the fire low in her belly that he'd been stoking all afternoon simply by existing.

"I want to taste you while you're standing." His voice was husky.

"Yes," she remembered to say, and moved her feet farther apart. "Oh, yes."

A kiss on her inner thigh. Another. His nose brushed her curls and she whimpered with need and impatience, moving her feet farther apart still to give him access.

His tongue flicked out and tasted her, and she jumped. Her labia were engorged and sensitive, ready and waiting for him. With his thumbs, he separated her folds and tasted her again, and the lovely slippery pleasure made her moan. And then his tongue was everywhere, tasting her, licking, finding her clitoris and sliding over it repeatedly until she thought she would scream. Then he changed his angle and she cried, "No, don't—" but his tongue slid into her vagina and stroked her from the inside and she thought she would collapse, it felt so wicked and so good.

"Please," she breathed, "I need you—"

Somehow he could drive her mad and understand pieces of sentences at the same time. He resumed his courtship of her clitoris, stroking her slowly at first, then faster, and the waves of pleasure fanned out while heat built at her very core. The biggest wave of all crested and crashed inside her, under the very spot where his tongue had created it, and she screamed and grabbed his head to push him away.

Too much—

Josh stood and caught her behind the shoulders and knees as her legs turned to rubber. This time there was no falling over, no laughter—his arms were strong and sure and determined as he picked her up and carried her the few steps to the bed.

Her body felt exhausted and energized at the same time, with an internal hunger that cried out for satisfaction.

"Fill me," she begged, pulling him down onto the duvet.

"One second." He stripped out of his clothes while she leaned on one elbow and enjoyed every inch of muscle and skin as he pulled off shirt and pants, underwear and socks. It took another second to get a condom out of the bedside table, two or three more to roll it on.

"Look at you," she said with admiration, taking him in her hand.

"Not exactly the Bomber."

"Thank God. Now, come here." She pulled him on top of her, his long, hard body satisfying the hunger in her skin that had gone begging all day. Her legs parted and the feel of his muscles against her soft inner thighs delighted her.

"Now," she urged him. "I need you inside me."

He probed her entrance once, twice. When she lifted her hips to bring him closer, he smiled at her impatience. His muscles bunched and he slid inside in one deep stroke.

Lauren threw her head back with a moan. When the entire length of him was sheathed tightly inside her, Josh looked into her face with eyes so dark with passion that they seemed to burn.

"Don't close your eyes," he whispered. "I want to really see you."

Lauren had made love before in daylight, but not with her eyes open. Allowing a man to see you naked was one thing. Allowing him into your body was another. But looking into his eyes as he made love to you? That was new and scary and intensely personal.

But he had such beautiful eyes, even more so now that they were so intently gazing at her, flickering in response to every sound she made.

And when they found that rhythm that built the pleasure of being filled into something deeper, more urgent, his breathing became shorter and hers found that rhythm, too. Finally he gasped, "L-Laur—" before he threw his head back and the convulsions of orgasm gripped him.

Lauren's body contracted around him, too, as his arms lost their ability to support him and he fell onto her. She wrapped her arms and legs around him, reveling in the way those muscles that were so strong could give way completely in the throes of pleasure. That he could lose himself so completely in her.

Trust her.

There was no getting around it, she thought as she held him close and felt his breathing become even and steady, though she knew he wasn't asleep.

Making love with your eyes open was a very scary thing.

*From Lorelei's blog*

One of the things we girls wonder about is the infamous locker room postmortem about the previous night's encounter—another place where trust comes in, isn't it? Can we really believe them when they say they don't talk about what we're like in bed? No names mentioned, of course. That wouldn't be sporting. But what about the details? Those can remain anonymous, right? Ha.

What would you do if, say, you were dating a reporter and he did an article that contained stuff you and he had done together? Now, if he wrote for the *Wall Street Journal* and you'd talked about investing in someone's company, that's one thing. But what if he worked for *Esquire* or some guy 'zine that talks about sex and religion and good clothes and all those things that matter to today's man? What then? The devil is in the details, darlings.

Lorelei

I have the right to remain silent. I just don't have the ability.

# 14

LATER THAT EVENING, Josh woke with a start at the sound of a soft voice out in the hall.

"Is it only eight-thirty? It feels like the middle of the night. I'm over at Josh's, so I thought I'd give you a heads-up in case Joanie wanted to stay over. Yes, probably. Well, I don't know…maybe I can upload while he's in the shower or something. No, of course he doesn't know. He is special, but he still doesn't need to know that. Tomorrow sometime, I guess. Okay. 'Bye."

He heard the chirp of a cell phone being turned off and then the soft pad of bare feet on the floor. Her body was a pale shadow in the dim light.

"We forgot dinner."

At the sound of his voice, she sucked in a breath and froze in the act of climbing into bed, then relaxed and snuggled down next to him. "I'm starving."

He slid an arm around her and she laid her head on his shoulder. "I can have a look in the fridge," he suggested. "Joanie Lam made a bunch of pot stickers for me a couple of weeks ago. They're still in the freezer. I have no idea what to do with them."

"Joanie gives you food?"

He smiled in the dark. "Yeah, she thinks I'm a helpless single guy who eats pizza every night."

"Are you?"

"My mom taught me how to cook. Basic stuff. Not pot stickers."

"Those are easy. Come on, let's go eat them."

She threw the covers back and he turned on the bedside lamp. Looked like she needed firsts on food before he got seconds on sex.

"Where are my—never mind. They're on your desk."

He pulled on shorts and jeans while she yanked on her T-shirt and the little skirt.

No bra. There might be seconds in his future after all.

Smiling, he padded barefoot into the kitchen and pulled the bag of little white dumplings out of the freezer. "What do you eat with these?"

"Veggies," she said firmly, and nudged him out of the way. "Let me have a look." She studied the interior of the fridge. "Exactly how long have you had those green beans?"

He thought for a moment. "Two weeks? Before the party at Clementine's."

She made a face and pulled the bag of decomposing pods out. "Get rid of 'em. Okay. Broccoli? Perfect. Onions? One onion. That'll do."

He chopped vegetables while she put the pot stickers in his best nonstick frying pan and poured in half an inch of water. "When the water boils away, then you put in a bit of oil and fry them."

"They have to be cooked twice? Seems like a lot of effort for not much return."

"Believe me, if Joanie is half the cook her girlfriend is, you'll get a return."

"Who's her girlfriend?"

"My roommate, Vivien, who is right up there on a par with my sister."

"And who's your sister?"

She gazed at him a moment while the dumplings bubbled behind her. "We really have to get caught up on the vital statistics, don't we? We went straight to sex and bypassed all the usual getting-to-know-you stuff."

He held up the knife in a position of surrender. "If you're going to cast flash relationships up to me again, I'm going out and getting that pizza."

The dumplings began to sizzle instead of bubble and she poured in a little oil and turned them all over.

"My sister is Aurora Constable."

"Constable? As in Lavender Field?"

"The very same. My other sister is Michaela Correlli. She's a child advocate."

"Right. I knew I'd heard her name before. Lorelei mentioned her not too long ago. After the key party. 'The beautiful and scary Michaela Correlli,' she called her. I wonder what your sister did to scare Lorelei? I wouldn't have thought it was possible."

A curtain of curly taffy hair prevented him from seeing her expression as she turned each dumpling over. The bottoms of the little triangular pastries were golden brown. His stomach rumbled.

"We'll never know," she said. "I didn't know you read 'On the Loose.'"

"I don't read the print column, just her blog. That's enough entertainment for me. She's getting a bit behind, though. She used to post every morning like clockwork, but it's been pretty sporadic this week."

"Maybe she got fired."

"Nah. *Inside Out* knows a good thing when they see it. John Garvey is still hot to find someone like her for *Left Coast*'s site." He glanced at her, but her hair was still in her face.

She shoveled the pot stickers onto a plate, crisp and glistening with oil, and put them in the oven to stay warm.

"Hand me those veggies, will you?" She stir-fried them with an experienced hand, and when they were done, they sat down to dinner.

He shook a little soy sauce onto a pot sticker and put it in his mouth. It was crisp, with a tender pork-and-vegetable filling.

"Man, these are good. I'm going to have to do some serious 'poor pitiful single me' whining in front of Joanie to get some more." Then his mind went back to what he'd been saying. "When we get this article put to bed, you should send John a proposal."

"What for?"

He enjoyed watching her eat. She treated every mouthful as a separate pleasure—even licking the oil from her lips.

"For a blog site. Not like Lorelei's per se—he wouldn't want her within ten miles of *Left Coast*. But I bet you'd be good at something like that."

She lowered her fork. "Why do you say that?"

"I don't know." Had he insulted her somehow? "You're smart, know a lot about high tech and lifestyles and social trends, and I never know what's going to come out of your mouth next."

"And this makes me a candidate to run a blog?"

"You'd give Lorelei a run for her money. You must read her, too. Sometimes the things you say remind me of her."

She dropped her fork on her empty plate and trapped his gaze with hers. "Sometimes the things you say remind me of sex." She got up and rounded the table with a long, stealthy stride like a stalking cat. "Have I told you lately that I love watching your mouth move?"

"Only a couple of days ag—urk!"

Obligingly, he lifted his hips as she tugged at his jeans. When she held him down and straddled him right there in the kitchen chair, he suddenly remembered that he hadn't seen her put her panties on when they'd gotten dressed. She was wet and swollen and her mouth was so hot as she lowered her body onto his that his brain cells sizzled into silence and he forgot all about Lorelei...and everything else.

WHEN LAUREN WOKE the next morning, she stared at the ceiling for a moment, disoriented. Her room at her apartment was pale pinkish yellow, the color of the sun slanting over the beach at the end of the day. A color that sounded horrid when she tried to describe it to the people at the paint store, but that she liked. It lifted her spirits, particularly on days when the fog socked in and rain melted through it.

These walls were cool and white and needed pictures and hangings on them in the worst way.

Josh's walls.

She turned to look at his pillow, but that side of the bed was empty. On her other side, on the bedside table sat a steaming mug with a sticky note affixed to the lamp next to it.

*Gone for a run. Back at 8:30.*

Propping herself up on her elbows, she peered across the bed at his clock. The digital numbers read 8:05. She threw back the duvet and yanked on her underwear, skirt and T-shirt. Twenty-five minutes to check her e-mail and upload something to Lorelei's blog. If Josh had noticed that her postings were sporadic, it was a sure bet her editor had noticed, too.

His computer was already booted up and, oh, joy, he

had a high-speed connection. In the time it took to take a swallow of her coffee, she was logged into her e-mail, where there were four—count 'em, four—messages from the Queen of Pain. The subject lines didn't look promising.

Blog uploads: two missing this week
Another blog upload missed
Meeting notice: review blog traffic
Request concall ASAP: blog

Lucky for her it was Saturday and the conference call wasn't until Monday, giving her two days to catch up on things. Her fingers moving swiftly, Lauren uploaded a stream-of-consciousness piece about CyberCon and responded to six or seven entries on her boards from Lynn and Karen, regulars who liked to riff on social themes and who were having a good time chewing on the "love at first sight" and "trust" threads. A couple of lines each to aristos5 and soozyboozy, two more regulars, and she was done.

Not a moment too soon. Steps sounded on the stairs outside and just as she closed all her screens, a key turned in the lock. By the time Josh shouldered open the door with a bakery box bearing a familiar lavender-and-green logo in his hands, she was standing by the window sipping coffee and admiring the view.

"I left the computer up in case you wanted to check e-mail." He put the box on the kitchen counter.

"Thanks. What's in there?"

"A couple of croissants with some kind of filling, and some fruit bread the girl said was good toasted with cream cheese. Unfortunately, all I have is butter."

"Butter's good. It took my sister months to come up

with that recipe. My favorites are the blueberry-and-cheese croissants, though."

He looked pleased. "That's what she said these were. Sounds weird to me but I took her word for it."

"Rory knows how to pick her staff. You can trust them when they recommend something."

He pulled a knife out of a drawer and cut some slices from the fruit bread. After he dropped them in the toaster, he put the croissants on a plate.

Watching him was like sipping a mocha espresso on a cold day. The way his hips moved, the way his running shorts pulled across his tight butt, the way his fingers touched the croissants without crushing the fragile layers of pastry. And now he stood waiting for the toaster with his weight on one leg and the opposite knee bent.

God, all she wanted to do was to run her hands all over him.

He looked up. "What?"

"How many times a week do women tell you you're beautiful?"

His hair fell forward the same way hers did when she wanted to hide something.

"Josh. Are you blushing?" With her coffee in one hand, she smoothed the tousled strands behind his ear with the other. "You are!"

The toast popped up and he busied himself buttering it. "Here. Eat your toast and quit asking goofy questions."

The hot fruit bread dripping in butter was divine. Almost as good as looking at him, but not as good as touching him.

"The girl was right," Josh said. "This is good."

"Here." She dabbed at the side of his mouth where

a particularly succulent berry had left a trace of juice. His tongue removed it and touched her finger, licking butter from its tip. His eyes ignited, holding hers and leaving no doubt that eating toast was not the uppermost priority on his mind. Her body responded simply to the tip of his tongue and those eyes—with him, it took so little, she thought in wonder. One look and desire puddled between her legs, deep down and hot.

"I need a shower," Josh said, his voice hushed with suggestion.

"Me, too," she replied a little breathlessly.

He took her hand and pulled her down the hall to the bathroom, where it didn't take them long to strip each other to the skin. He turned on the shower while kicking his shorts out of the way—who said that men couldn't multitask?—and dragged her into the glass enclosure with him.

Hot water cascaded all around them as she locked her arms around his neck and gave him the full-body kiss she'd been craving since she'd awakened to find him gone. This wasn't sleepy morning sex, with her mind half awake and her body still asleep and unaroused, as it had been with some of the men she'd been with. This was Josh, hot and urgent and irresistible, seducing her every time he moved. Making her think about kissing every time he spoke. Filling her mind the way he filled her body, crowding out every sensation except the ones he created with those magic hands and that sinful mouth.

Slick as a seal, with water splashing off his shoulders and streaming from his hair in runnels, Josh turned her around and held her in front of him, his eager erection probing her derriere as he cupped her breasts from close behind.

"You're so sexy," he murmured over the rush of water. "I love to follow you and watch you walk." His engorged penis slid between her legs and she arched her back. "The way your skirt swings, the way the muscles flex in your calves." She braced both hands on the wet tiles and tilted her rear up to give him better access. "It makes me think about doing this," he growled.

She was so hot for him she could hardly stand it. "Josh," she moaned. She'd wanted a talker, hadn't she? Now that she had one, she wished he'd stop and give her what she desperately needed.

He slid the shower door open wide enough to reach out and grab a condom out of a drawer. After rolling it on, he slid his hands around her and snugged her up against him.

She cried out with satisfaction as he entered her. He stroked her from within in a way that made her hotter than she'd ever been. Because he was standing up, his strokes were shorter, exciting, giving her pleasure in new places. The sweet pressure built and then just when she thought she would explode with it, he reached around and found her clitoris with his fingers. Already primed and wet, Lauren felt as though two powerful currents connected—ignited—

She cried out as pleasure exploded inside her, felt Josh hold her even closer with his free arm as he shuddered against her back in the heights of his own orgasm.

They stood, shaking, under the hot spray for a moment, then Josh slid out of her limp body and reached for the soap. Gently, he soaped a cloth hanging on the rail and washed her back and shoulders, moved to her hips, then each trembling leg. He paid special attention to the area between her legs, using his hands instead of the cloth so he wouldn't irritate the sensitized, swollen flesh.

Far from irritation, Lauren's knees buckled a little as his soapy fingers slid and rubbed.

"Josh, I'm going to—"

She came again against his fingers, holding on to the wall of the shower while she shivered in delight. Lauren wondered a little deliriously if one body could take so many different kinds of pleasure. She practically purred as he cupped water in his hands and rinsed her clean.

"My turn," she said when she was able to speak.

She soaped the cloth and gave him the same treatment, part bath and part massage, outlining the planes of his body with her hands and marveling that some gorgeous female hadn't snapped him up long ago. Then she shut that thought out. Nothing was going to spoil the moment.

Down his legs and back up again, paying special attention to his scrotum and penis, which even now was still at half mast.

Once they were rinsed off, they dried each other with the same care. Josh staggered into the bedroom and fell on the bed.

"I'd better start taking vitamins," he told the ceiling. "I haven't had this much exercise in—" he glanced at her as she crawled in beside him on the bed "—a long time."

The duvet folded around them as she cuddled into his side. Her body was singing with satisfaction and she was as close as she'd ever been to being perfectly happy. "Why not? How can a man like you still be single?"

She thought she'd make him blush again, but instead he considered her question seriously.

"Because I bail," he said in a tone that was soft with honesty. "We start out having a good time, doing things together, and then when it starts to get personal, like I find out she has some dark secret or some problem she needs to work out, I find I can't get involved."

"Can't or won't?"

"Won't, I guess. I was in a relationship a few years ago with the woman who owns the Vargas Vineyards. She was the most high-maintenance person I've ever met. It took me a long time to realize that *high mainte-nance* is just another word for *selfish.* But by then I was too exhausted to think." He cocked an eyebrow at her. "I know you're not selfish. Or high maintenance. You don't have any dark secrets, do you?"

For a split second she considered telling him about Lorelei, and then she heard his voice in her mind saying John Garvey wouldn't want Lorelei within ten miles of the magazine. Josh probably wouldn't, either. This was too new and she was too happy to spoil it by having him think badly of her because she worked for a mouthy, take-no-prisoners tabloid.

"I went to a creative briefing with no panties on once," she said lightly.

"Oh, my God." He rolled up on one elbow to look at her. "That *is* dark. What were you doing, seducing your client?"

"No." She gave a regretful sigh. "I just forgot to do the laundry, that's all. I had to run out at lunch and buy a pair."

He chuckled and lay back on the bed, gathering her closer. "That's what I like about you. You look so inno-cent, with your curly hair and pretty face, and then you turn it all upside down by doing something wicked."

"Nobody knew about it," she protested.

"You knew." He rolled over and kissed her. "And now I know. Just in case I ever need something to blackmail you with."

I was at a party the other night where someone wondered whether talking on message boards was the same thing as forming a flash mob. This person suggested that people who do this kind of stuff are just afraid to commit. To activism. To each other. To themselves. What do you think? I'm not talking about drive-by posters, I'm talking about you guys, the regulars, who come together in huge numbers to say your bit and then disappear until next time.

Do you think we're the literary equivalent of a flash mob? Or is it more like a big coffeehouse where the java is free and everyone is listening? Is anyone listening? Do we really listen? Or are we too busy posting, shouting our word, hoping for our fifteen minutes of fame?

Lorelei

# 15

BLACKMAIL?

*Okay, Cinderella, when they start talking about blackmail it's time to call the coach and get out of the palace.*

Lauren slid off the bed and reached for her clothes. They'd already been off and on twice this morning. It was a wonder her jersey skirt wasn't stretched into something she could wash her car with.

*Just get them on and get out of here.*

"Lauren?" Josh sat up. "I was only joking."

"I know." She gave him the best smile she could muster. "But I have a lot of work to do on...on the article and I need to get started."

"Do it here. We're supposed to be collaborating, remember?"

"I can e-mail you my stuff when it's finished and you can add the technical side."

"That isn't collaborating, that's serial boredom." He rolled off the mattress. "Come on. I have a network here. You can use my laptop and I'll use the computer, and we'll build the article simultaneously."

She pulled her T-shirt over her head and stared at him. "How?"

"I have this nifty software called 'Swizzle.' I'm beta testing it for one of my—friends. It treats a document as a chatroom so two people can work on it at once without erasing each other's work."

In spite of her urge to run, Lauren found herself getting interested. "Swizzle?"

"Yeah, like 'mix together.' The real acronym is SWSL, Simultaneous WorkSpace Language, but that doesn't pop very well on the packaging. Come on, I'll show you."

Swizzle, ha. More like swindle. She was being talked into staying, and worse, she was starting to like it. Lauren held out until he had fired up both computers and was demonstrating how they could write the article together while he sat at his desk and she slouched on his comfortable couch with his laptop in her lap. Then she caved completely.

"So, is our theme still rejection?" he asked as a fresh document space loaded.

"Or the natural inclination to avoid it." Lauren thought for a moment, then began the first paragraph. After that, it was like a dance. She broached an idea or commented on an aspect of human need or desire that the products filled—focusing on Amity and the flirtatious role-playing game at first—and Josh backed it up with his knowledge of how the technology worked. For the role-playing game, his knowledge went particularly deep.

Way too deep for a fifteen-minute interview at CyberCon.

"How do you know all this stuff about *Contact?*" she finally asked, visions of young women in red tank tops dancing in her head.

"I used to date one of the cofounders." His fingers flashed on the keys as she watched, fascinated. In another century he would have been a honky-tonk piano player in some Western bar, his hands moving over the keyboard with just that long-fingered grace. She could practically see the cigarette hanging from his lips and the derby hat pushed back on his head.

She blinked and the vision cleared. "Maddie." *I knew it.*

"Yeah. Maddie Matsumoto. Brilliant woman." He glanced up at her. "It was a couple of years ago. She got busy trying to fund her game and I got busy with the magazine, so we parted ways." The words he'd been typing appeared in her copy of the document. "Do you want to add anything before I start talking about the interface?"

Lauren bit back a comment about his unwillingness to open up about the beautiful Maddie Matsumoto. Fine. She could take a hint.

"Yeah. Give me a couple of minutes. I already covered female and male modes of play, but I had some more thoughts about the whole interlocking relationships thing. And I need a segue into the NeuraLove suit."

"It'd be nice to get a quote from a soldier on that. It's not the Bomber, but the theory is the same."

"Do you have any contacts in the military?"

"No, but John does. He was a sergeant back in the day. I'll make some calls on Monday."

When three or four hours had gone by, Lauren realized they were in "the zone," that place journalists love where the ideas came so fast you can hardly get them down. It was like being in a jazz band, Lauren imagined, playing music where you knew only the tune, and the rhythm, the chords, the background fabric was improvised and made up wherever it all fit the best.

It was like sex.

Two people might know all the moves separately, but bringing their knowledge to each other to create something new and fabulous was what it was all about.

Sex with Josh was pretty damn fabulous. Writing with him was all that, too.

So what was the matter with taking him a little more seriously and not running for cover every time he said or did something she didn't like? He was an individual, and he couldn't scrub every word before it came out of his mouth. So he'd had a relationship with Maddie Matsumoto. She would just have to deal. He was with her, Lauren, now, and it wasn't Maddie he had made love with three times in twelve hours.

The guy was famous for his bone-scraping honesty and cynical humor in print, but never once had he turned it on her to hurt or humiliate. Well, there was the whole Lacey thing, but she could see now that he had used the material he'd had on hand to underpin his story's thesis, not to launch a personal attack on her.

She was just too damn sensitive when it came to letting people into her life. Deep down she was afraid they'd say they loved her and then leave anyway, the way Dad and Mom and Luis and Carl had.

But Emma hadn't. She'd said, "I love you and I'll always be here for you, no matter what," and she'd meant it. Mikki and Rory were fiercely loyal. Mikki had even decked a local bully the first year Lauren had gone to school with her new foster sisters. He'd made the mistake of calling Lauren a crack ho, and he'd paid for it with five stitches and a cap on his front tooth.

Richie Mancuso, that had been his name. Last she'd heard he was in the city attorney's office. Hmm. Maybe Lorelei could start reminiscing about painful high-school memories. If what Rory said was true, maybe the pen could jab as well as Mikki's right fist.

"What are you smiling about?" Josh put a grilled-cheese sandwich and a bowl of salsa and chips on the coffee table in front of her. "Finishing the marathon?"

"No, just making a note to myself about—" She stopped just in time. "About an article possibility for later," she finished a little lamely.

Geez. Until she was seriously talking employment with *Left Coast,* she wasn't going to say anything about being Lorelei. Once they were formally interviewing her, of course, she would have to include it as part of her résumé. All she needed to do was to make sure John Garvey was the guy doing the interviewing, and maybe Tina Bianchi, who seemed very supportive and with whom she at least had a common interest in vintage clothes. John seemed to respect Lorelei's results, if not her methods. But until then, she wasn't going to indulge in pillow talk about her alter ego, and that meant keeping her a secret from Josh.

For now.

She'd deal with his opinions of Lorelei later, when their relationship was a little more solid.

Because, she realized, she wanted it to be solid. An odd feeling bloomed under her breastbone, the same feeling she got when she saw Josh walk into a room.

She'd not only talked herself into not running away, she'd talked herself into moving forward.

Toward him.

WHEN THE FIRST DRAFT of the story, which they were calling "Love is Virtually All You Need," was completed and all that was left was some fact checking and maybe a telephone interview with a soldier, Josh sat back and grinned at Lauren.

"I don't know about you, but I need to get out of here."

"I need to go home and get out of these clothes. Borrowing your deodorant is all very well, but I draw the line at your toothbrush."

"You can use my toothbrush if you want." He waved an arm at the living room, the kitchen and the view of the Golden Gate Bridge out his front window. "Or anything else."

"Josh. I have to go home."

"Okay." He gathered up the pile of brochures, her clips and the research material they'd downloaded from the Internet. "How about I drive you home, you change, and we go get something to eat?"

"And after that?"

"We can come back here if you want. Or not. It's up to you."

She tilted her head and narrowed her eyes at him. "Are we nesting?"

"Uh…I have no idea. What's that?"

"It's the step that happens after courtship and sex. It's packing an overnight bag that turns into a toothbrush in each house that turns into sets of clothes in the spare closet. It's a slippery slope, is what it is."

"You've really got this social customs thing down to a science, haven't you?"

"It's what people do."

"But is it what we do?"

"Is there a 'we'?"

He paused and tapped the stack of paper and brochures together. "If that's what you want."

*Don't push. Take it slow.*

If he got past the "let's talk about my problems" point, this was the point at which he absolutely, without fail, bailed. The infamous "are we a couple" question had frightened braver men than he. And yet the thought of going his own way and not seeing Lauren anymore just made him think of fog and rainy windows and being alone.

Being alone had never bothered him before. After Elena, he'd been happy enough with work relationships and camaraderie with guys like John Garvey and some of the venture capitalists with whom he did a lot of work. Sure, there had been Maddie and a couple of casual girlfriends, but he'd kept things that way—casual. He'd never felt the urge to nest.

"Josh," Lauren said patiently, "this isn't about what I want. It's about what we want."

"Are you going to dump me again?" The question popped out of his mouth before his brain had time to couch it a little less bluntly.

She looked down and her cheeks took on a little color. Look at that. Without even trying, he'd made her blush.

"Because, you know, my bathroom's pretty small. If I'm going to take the plunge and move some of my stuff out of the way so you can put your toothbrush there, I want some assurance that you're not going to call it quits in the middle of a conversation and disappear."

"No," she said in a low tone. "I'm not going to dump you." Her voice took on more strength. "I was upset about the article and had this dumb idea that I was going to seduce you and then leave you wanting more."

"Which you did." He'd been so dazzled by her it hadn't even occurred to him that she might have an ulterior motive. They'd both made their mistakes. He'd been dumb enough to use his own experience with her in that article, knowing she'd probably read it.

And while they were being honest, he should probably tell her the real connection between himself and the magazine and Maddie and her game. It wasn't as if she would go and announce that he wasn't just a freelancer to everybody at the *Left Coast* office. She wouldn't lose respect for him the way some of the journalists who competed with him might.

"But it backfired on me," she confessed, more cheerfully. "Once a woman gets a taste of you, it's hard to walk away."

"Didn't you compare me to a truffle once?"

"I still do."

"Do you think I'm bad for you?"

"Truffles can be nutritious. Think of the calcium you get in milk chocolate."

She grinned and he couldn't help but grin back. She practically sparkled with good humor and satisfaction for a job well done on their story. Not to mention the sex. That gave a kind of velvety texture to her skin and sensuality to her movements that hadn't been there before.

The moment for true confessions passed. He'd tell her later. Right now it didn't seem as important as seeing where she lived. "Come on, then. If I can't keep you naked all the time, then I guess we'll have to go get you some clothes."

When they got there sometime later, he saw that her apartment was nothing special, just a two-bedroom in a Marina building that looked like thousands of others.

"You say your roommate is dating Joanie Lam? That's quite a coincidence." He wandered around a living room that sported a bookshelf packed with books, a huge silk fan on the wall and a pile of embroidered cushions on the couch.

"Not really," she called from the bedroom, where he heard drawers opening and shutting. "They met at the key party, the same as we did. Viv traded her lock with a gay guy's key and got a lucky match."

He gazed at an eight-by-ten photo in an ornate silver frame on the bookcase. It was Lauren, a dark-haired woman and Aurora Constable, whom he recognized from publicity photos for her bakeries. The three sisters, he guessed, seated on a sand dune somewhere and backlit by the long reddish rays of late afternoon. Their hair was tossed by the wind and Aurora's head was thrown back in laughter. They looked as though they shared some huge joke just between the three of them—and they weren't about to share it with the photographer or the viewer.

A dart of longing shot through him. The only photographs he had of himself and his parents had been taken back when he was in elementary school, when they could still be called a family. He couldn't imagine trying to schedule a photography session between Dad's business trips, his own hours and Mom's charity work. They'd have to do it on a Sunday, when—

"Lauren?"

"I'm almost done."

"What are you doing tomorrow night?"

She emerged from the bedroom with a pink leather carryall, wearing khaki shorts and a salmon-pink T-shirt. "Having wild sex on your dining room table?" she said hopefully.

"Now there's a thought. Hold on to it. How'd you like to have dinner with me and my parents?"

The carryall dropped to the floor with a thud. "Wow. Moving a little fast, aren't we?"

"You know, meeting-the-parents isn't the social rite

of passage that it is in the movies. I have dinner with them every Sunday. I want to be with you. Ergo, that means that in a perfect world where I get what I want, either I blow them off completely or you come to dinner with me."

"Blowing them off sounds good." When he didn't reply, she eyed him. "Every Sunday?"

"Yep. My dad even schedules his trips so he doesn't miss it. Which is weird, because he never bothered to when I was growing up."

"Maybe he realized his mistake."

"I think he just likes roast beef."

She collected her purse from the couch, where she'd tossed it earlier, and turned with an air of taking the plunge, no matter the cost. "I would love to go to Sunday dinner with your parents. That means, of course, that you have to come to Saturday brunch with my mom and sisters."

He had an odd feeling that was like inviting a Christian to the Coliseum to see the lions. "Sure," he said bravely. "Fair's fair."

They ate dinner at a little Italian hole-in-the-wall in North Beach, then went back to his condo to watch Arnold Schwarzenegger and Jamie Lee Curtis save the world, their daughter and their marriage in *True Lies*.

"I've seen this thirty times at least, and love it every time," Lauren confided as she slipped the movie into the DVD player.

They fell asleep with the window open and for once the night stayed clear and cool, which meant it would be sunny in the morning. Josh's sleepy prediction turned out to be correct, so they spent the day at Half Moon Bay wandering through the farmer's market collecting lunch and then taking their booty to San Gregorio Beach for a picnic.

Josh couldn't remember the last time he'd bought food in a farmer's market. In fact, he knew he hadn't. And as for eating sourdough bread and briny olives and thick slices of cheese with his feet buried in the sand and his back against a log, well, that was a first, too.

"Is there such a thing as a picnic virgin?" He swallowed the last of his bread and cheese and washed it down with a mouthful of a terrific Merlot from—he picked up the bottle and glanced at the label. Look at that. Vargas Vineyards.

Silently he toasted Elena, who had finally given him something.

Lauren eyed him curiously. "Please tell me you've been on a picnic before."

"I can't. I've been rewinding my life and I can't remember one, ever. Do you know how sad that is?"

"What did your family do for vacations?"

"We went to places where my dad had sales meetings. The company flew him there, so he only had to pay for two tickets. Of course, it meant Mom and I were on our own most of the time, but she's a very capable person. She'd have a folder full of stuff to go and see, whether it was Orlando or New Orleans or Santa Fe."

"Every holiday was a learning experience?"

"More or less."

"But what about the fun part? You know, goofing off in the pool, going to the beach, hiking?"

"I imagine we did some of that, too, but what seems to have stuck in my head is the fact that the Palace of Governors is the only original building left in Santa Fe's main square." Which was pretty sad, when you got right down to it. "What about you?"

Lauren gazed into the distance, where a flock of sandpipers were playing tag with the creamy surf. "No."

"No picnics, either?"

"Not until I came to Emma's. She might live in town but her heart is out in the country. She has these goofy chickens on her kitchen curtains." She shook her head and smiled. "Anyway. There used to be a widow's walk on top of our house, but when she had the roof redone a couple of years ago it had to come down. I remember thinking she was either the weirdest person on the planet or the most wonderful. She made this fabulous meal and we carted it up three flights of stairs and ate it on the widow's walk, up above the city." Lauren's voice was soft with memory. "It was just about this time of year— Memorial Day—and I ate sausages and tomatoes in oil and big wheels of homemade sourdough bread and watched the fireworks explode over the bay practically at eye level." Her voice trembled and Josh realized with a sudden rush of compassion that she was crying. "She…she and my sisters gave me the most beautiful moment I'd ever had. That's when I knew I had a home and a family, and I wasn't going to give them up for anything."

He slid his arm around her and pulled her close as his own throat closed up with a sudden sense of loss. He had a home and a family, but beautiful, defining moments fashioned out of pure love had been—and still were—few and far between.

In fact, more of them had been packed into a week with Lauren than he could remember experiencing in a year.

*Change,* the fortune teller's voice whispered in his memory. *Remember the Ace of Wands.*

And there had been something about focusing will and intention and keeping things balanced as energy went from the old to the new.

Maybe there was something in it after all.

*From Lorelei's blog*

All this week the big draw at the Santa Clara Convention Center is CyberCon, the virtual reality and cybersex show. Much more interesting than employment fairs or Comdex, it's pulling in crowds like the convention center has never seen.

You, too, can see the latest in e-mail bots, V.R. lovers, cyberdildonics—go on, look it up. I dare you— and the NeuraLove suit, which redefines "slipping into something more comfortable." The next best thing to being there.

What does this wild variety of technology have in common? Could it be that we're turning to the interface and the mouse because we can't get what we need in person? Because we get satisfaction without expending all the effort of going through the rejections, working out dates, asking for a commitment…all that relationship stuff.

It kind of makes you wonder if the point of relationship is sexual satisfaction or, well, relationship, doesn't it?

Lorelei

Never knock at death's door. Ring the doorbell and run, he hates that.

# 16

SOMETHING IN THE construction of Mrs. McCrae's dining-room chairs prevented Lauren from getting comfortable or attempting to relax. They were beautiful chairs, Queen Anne style with petit point seat covers, but her shoulders were beginning to ache.

Or maybe it was just the company.

The transition between a beautiful picnic on the beach and their subsequent lovemaking at Josh's place to this cold, formal dining room was literally making her hurt. She wondered how Josh felt.

Mr. McCrae—he had been introduced as James but Lauren couldn't imagine ever calling him that—sat at the head of the table, carving the roast. Beside him, Irene McCrae twisted the string of pearls at her throat, then patted them into place on her baby-blue cashmere sweater.

"Some Yorkshire pudding, Lauren?"

Mr. McCrae put a slice of beef on her plate and Irene passed a bowl containing muffin-size puffs of dough. Surreptitiously, Lauren watched Josh melt a pat of butter in his, then dropped one into her own. Did Rory know about Yorkshire pudding? Lauren had never heard of it before tonight.

The salad was a work of art, crisp and loaded with enough different kinds of veggies to stock a supermarket shelf. And the asparagus swam in a tangy sauce that probably held a thousand calories per spoonful.

"What kind of sauce is on the asparagus, Mrs. Mc-Crae?" she asked, enjoying a mouthful.

"Hollandaise. It's fussy, though, you have to watch it or it separates."

"It's delicious." *Fattening.* Irene must work out if she cooked this way all the time. The woman couldn't weigh more than one twenty, and you could crease paper on her cheekbones.

"Thank you, dear. So, Joshua tells us you met recently?"

*Yup, at a key party. It was completely random. Oh, and he made me come up against the dining-room wall.*

"Yes, at a charity event a couple of weeks ago. And then we went to the S.F.S.J. Black on White Ball, as well."

"Are you active in charity work?"

*Uh, no, I'm active in earning a paycheck.* "No, but the cause was one I support."

"And what was that?" Mr. McCrae asked, dabbing his lips with his napkin.

"It was a fund-raiser for Baxter House, a transitional home for girls in the foster care system."

"A worthy cause." Irene cut her asparagus into one-inch diagonals with her knife.

"That Maureen Baxter isn't your usual social worker." Mr. McCrae stabbed a knife into his pudding and sliced it in two, then poured gravy on it. "Every time I go to one of my shareholders' meetings it seems she's there, asking for donations."

Lauren swallowed a mouthful of asparagus. The sauce was so rich it was losing its flavor with every bite. "She supports a number of causes, but Baxter House is the one closest to her heart. She came out of the foster care system, too."

"Too?" Irene inquired.

Her mother, Emma, might look like the perpetually calm image of the earth mother, but her convictions were as strong as tectonic movement and her courage immense. All of the values that she'd managed to instill in her daughters seemed to come together like a laser beam in Lauren's mind, just for this moment.

"Yes. I was in the foster care system, myself. My father left us when I was a child, and when my mom's heroin habit got to the point where she couldn't care for me, Child Protective Services took over."

"Heroin habit?" Irene repeated faintly.

Lauren threw down the truth like an opera glove. "Yes. She'd been using for years, but it got to the point where there was no money and no food—no apartment, either, we were evicted—and she was strung out most of the time. So contrary to what many believe, C.P.S. was the best thing that happened to me."

"Evicted?" Mr. McCrae repeated.

"I lucked out. Some kids find situations that are nearly as miserable as the ones they left, but I got Emma. She specialized in teenagers, the ones people don't like to take." Lauren grinned. "My sister Michaela was every foster mother's nightmare, but she met her match in Emma Constable."

"Emma Constable?" McCrae dug into his roast beef again. "On Garrison Street?"

Lauren eyed him. "Yes. Do you know her?"

McCrae snorted. "Do I know her. Everyone in real estate knows her. If not for her, Garrison Street would be a modern housing and shopping district instead of a row of tumbledown sticks."

*Sticks,* Lauren had learned as a teenager, were what San Franciscans called the decorative Victorian houses built in the late 1900s, with a lot of wood overlay, cornices and painted trim. Emma's house wasn't as spectacular as some, but it wasn't the dump he made it out to be, either.

"Dad, the people who live in sticks love them," Josh said. "They'd have no reason to want a modern housing district if they're living in a house where they're happy."

"Garrison Street isn't tumbledown," Lauren added. "Well-lived-in, maybe. It seemed like a palace to me when I first came."

Where she'd had her own room with its cubbyholes and narrow window, and where there was more food in the kitchen than she had seen in one place in years. And where there was love in every inch. Oh, yes, Garrison Street had been a palace, all right. Still was.

"That property is worth a fortune, but she won't sell. And worse, she got all the neighbors together to form some kind of consortium against development. Stupid woman."

"Dad," Josh said sharply. Under cover of the damask tablecloth, he took her hand and squeezed it in support.

Lauren's squeezed back, then released his hand and put down her fork. "Mr. McCrae, that stupid woman is my mother. The one who saved my life in the most literal sense."

"You owe Lauren an apology, Dad." Josh backed her up without hesitation, and she wondered just what kind of relationship they had. At the moment it seemed more like combatants than father and son.

McCrae laid his fork down, as if he, too, was squaring off for battle. "Apology for what?" he demanded.

"I'm just stating facts. All those people have been offered fair market value for their houses. More than fair. They could relocate and get twice the square footage they have now. But no. Because of one stubborn woman they all lose."

"I don't think it's a loss to stay in the home you and your family have been in since the turn of the century," Lauren pointed out. "Mrs. Delaney came to her house as a bride in 1948." Mrs. Delaney was the last daughter of the Nob Hill Delaneys. Lauren couldn't imagine her moving to a rancher out in the flatlands of the Central Valley just because some developer wanted the fifty-by-eighty-foot lot the house stood on.

"It is if the house is falling down around you."

"That was the point of the consortium, you know, Mr. McCrae. A pool of money for repairs and restoration."

"No, it wasn't. She got them all to agree not to sell."

"I'm afraid you're mistaken."

"Miss Massey," he said with heavy patience, looking over his glasses, "that's a very commendable motive, but I'm afraid people don't just pool their money to repair other people's houses."

"Yes, they do," she retorted. "And they donate free labor, too. I even learned how to operate a nail gun." Which she could use about now on someone's stubborn head.

He stared at her for a moment, then obviously decided it wasn't worth the argument. He picked up his knife and fork and sawed at his beef.

"We're still waiting for that apology." Josh dropped the reminder into the silence like a stone into a pool.

"I'm not going to apologize for my opinions," McCrae said shortly.

"Even if they're rude to my guest and based on faulty data?"

"Josh, I don't know why you think this is any of your—"

Irene put down her knife on her Minton plate with a clatter. "James Randall McCrae, you apologize to Lauren this instant," she admonished. "Do you think Josh would allow someone to call me stupid? What is the matter with you?"

McCrae stared at his wife. "What, are you ganging up on me, too?"

"No one is ganging up on you. But I do expect certain standards of behavior at this table, and politeness to our son's guests is one of them." A moment passed. "James?"

He rolled his eyes and then tossed a glance of disgust Lauren's way. "I apologize."

"Accepted," she said. "Could I have another Yorkshire pudding, please?"

"AND THE CONGRESSIONAL medal of valor goes to Lauren Massey, for courage under fire." Josh closed the door of his boyhood bedroom and hugged Lauren from behind. Her spine seemed to wilt and she laid her head back against his shoulder.

"Has anyone ever told your dad he's a jerk?"

"Probably not in so many words, but I finished high school early and went to U.C.L.A. Three guesses why."

"You didn't want to live at home until you were thirty?"

"I didn't even want to live at home until I was thirteen. When I was ten, I asked my aunt if I could come and be *her* son."

She turned in his arms and gave him a full body hug, as if to make up for hugs that might have gone missing in the past. "How does your mom put up with it?"

"She's learned how to handle him. I never could, which is why I got out. But I've never seen her take him on in front of company. Usually she reads him the riot act when they're behind closed doors. Either both of us have a real low tolerance today, or we both like you."

"I'm grateful for your support," she said. "I would have hated to throw down my fork and storm out, which was Plan B."

"You could have gone with Plan C, let it slide."

"Letting is slide isn't the right thing to do. It just means they get away with it."

Lauren was looking at his swimming trophy on the bookcase, and he followed her gaze. Neither fingerprint nor dust marred its glossy surface, thanks to the cleaners his mother had come in twice a week. It surprised him that they bothered with his old room, though. He certainly didn't spend any time here, but maybe Mom did. Did her smooth, manicured hand ever hesitate over the phone while she debated whether to invite him to lunch? he wondered. Did she ever want to throw on a pair of jeans and suggest a picnic?

Maybe he should surprise her one of these days and ask her himself.

"As a kid I learned to pick my battles," he told Lauren softly. "Now I only see them once a week, and we have lively discussions about the weather and what's on top of the *New York Times*'s book list."

"I didn't know you were a swimmer." She indicated the trophy and the ribbons. "That must be where the nice shoulders came from."

He snorted. "That must be where brainy guys go who don't make it onto the football or basketball teams."

"Football is overrated. I'd rather have a guy with

nice arms and shoulders than someone with stress fractures in ninety-eight percent of his body." She tilted her head to study the spines of the books below the trophy. "*Prince Valiant?* And *Star Wars?*"

"And later *The Sword of Shannara* and *Lord Foul's Bane*."

"Into quest epics, were we?"

He smiled and ran an affectionate finger over the cracked spines of the paperbacks. "I think it was more the notion that one guy could change the world if he had the right equipment. Maybe that's why I went into journalism instead of getting an M.D. like Dad wanted."

"Has he forgiven you?"

Josh shrugged. "I'm thirty-two years old. It's not up to him to forgive or not. I live my life the way that makes me happy. Come on, let's get out of here. I keep telling Mom she should turn this room into a study or something. It's not like I'm coming back."

She followed him out into the hall and pointed at the flight of stairs to the third floor at the end. "What's up there?"

"It changes. One year it was a weight room. Then my mom got into quilting and she had giant piles of fabric and big frames in there. It was where we had my birthday parties when I was a kid."

"Come on. I want to see."

When they got to the top of the stairs Lauren looked over the rail, but there was nothing but a big, empty room that extended over a good half of the topmost floor.

"Looks like they're between crazes," Josh commented.

Up here it was still warm from the heat of the day, and silent.

"It smells like my mom's house." Lauren breathed in the scent of old wood and furniture polish. "That is, when she isn't lending rooms to her down-and-out friends who smell like Patch or dirty socks. And it isn't all color-coordinated like this."

That was his mom, color-coordinated to the nth degree. The paint on the window frames and wainscoting was a tasteful gray, blended to bring out the hunter green of the walls, even up here where there was hardly any traffic.

But he was less interested in what the third floor smelled like than the warm scent of Lauren's perfume as it rose from her skin to tantalize him. His chest brushed her shoulder blades where she stood peering through the rail. When she stepped back to go downstairs again, he didn't move.

Instead he slid an arm around her waist and held her in place against the banister. Though the overhead light was on in the big work space, it didn't reach the stairwell except in slices between the posts of the rail. But who needed light to see by when all your other senses—smell, taste and touch—were working just fine?

"How quiet can you be?" he breathed in her ear, then nibbled her earlobe.

"We could go in your room," she whispered.

Hot, dark blood rushed into his groin at the way she got his meaning instantly and he pressed himself against the curves of her derriere.

"Can't wait that long."

Just thinking about making love where someone could open the door below them at any second felt illicit and delicious.

"I can be really quiet," she promised him in a whisper over her shoulder.

She was wearing a royal-blue silk sheath that looked as though it might have come from the Far East. He smoothed both hands down her ribs, the slick fabric picking up the heat from her skin beneath it. "I didn't know you had discovery fantasies."

"I just discovered them," she breathed, her cheek dimpling with a wicked smile.

He cupped her breasts in both hands through the fabric and felt her nipples harden in response through both bra and silk. She reached behind and traced his erection through the fabric of his pants with both hands, which arched her back and forced her breasts more firmly into his palms.

The soft curve where her neck and shoulder met begged for his mouth. He dropped kisses all along that curve, breathing in her scent and loving the way her breath shortened and hitched. His belt buckle jingled briefly and then fell silent as she tackled the button on his waistband. When it popped free, she grinned, then turned to face him and pulled the zipper down.

"Let's see how good you are at keeping quiet," she whispered. He sucked in a breath as her hands dove into the waistband of his shorts and she sheathed his cock with her fingers. "Remember, not a sound."

She eased his gray flannel trousers and his shorts down his legs, then moved down one stair, where she knelt. As she nuzzled the hollow in his thigh where it met his groin, his eager penis bobbed.

"Did you bring protection?" she murmured against his skin.

He had forgotten how to talk. "No," he rasped. Condoms weren't usually necessary when he had dinner with his parents, but then, with Lauren he should have known better. Condoms were likely to be necessary at any time of the day or night, and in any place.

"Guess I'll have to wait until later. Lovely thought." Her voice, muffled as she breathed on his skin and nibbled her way down a long muscle in his thigh, held both promise and a kind of triumphant laughter.

She took him in her mouth then, and he grabbed the railing for support as his knees wobbled. Her tongue encircled the engorged head of his penis, rapid swirls that pulled him into a tornado of sensation intensified by the roaring of his own blood in his ears.

How was it possible for a woman to be so giving? Every time he was with Lauren, it seemed, she gave part of herself to him. Whether it was her writing talent, her body, her memories, it didn't matter—she shared them with him without thought for what she might get out of the deal.

The fact that they could be discovered at any second seemed to have put his body's responses in the fast lane. Every sensation arrowed down to where her mouth, pliant and demanding, met his body, urgent and giving. The tornado of pleasure built, and when she reached for his testicles to massage them at just the right moment, the tornado turned into a rush of pleasure that roared out of the depths of him.

He gritted his teeth and tried not to cry out her name while his throat worked and his body spasmed in pleasure. She ran her hands up the backs of his naked thighs and milked him with those clever lips, drawing his climax out until the last possible moment.

Then it was she who pulled his briefs and trousers up again, zipping and buckling everything back in place while he lay against the banister breathing as heavily as if he'd just run up all three flights of stairs.

"Come here," he said at last, and sat on one of the steps. She sat between his legs one step below and he wrapped his arms around her and dipped his head to whisper in her ear. "I'll never look at these stairs the same way again."

"You mean you've never done this before?" She nuzzled the damp vee of skin in the open collar of his shirt, smiling.

"Are you kidding? Any girl I might have brought here didn't last until dessert." He paused while his breathing and heart rate slowed almost to normal. "They must have had lousy time management skills. Forgotten appointments were always coming up."

She chuckled into his shirtfront. "I don't scare easily."

"I noticed that."

"But I just remembered an appointment."

He closed his eyes in fake disappointment and groaned. "I knew it. At least you hung around for the cheesecake."

"I make a point of never missing dessert." She kissed him, a long thank-you kiss that included a lot of tongue and sped up their breathing again. "So let's go back to your place for my turn."

*From Lorelei's blog*

If you're feeling a little out of touch and the thought of a flash mob just doesn't do it for you, you really shouldn't miss CyberCon. I mean it. Where else on the planet can you be totally sexually stimulated while not exchanging a single word with another person? Of course, I've had boyfriends like that, but we're not talking about me. We're talking about what in human nature would drive it to create technology for sex, completely bypassing that evolutionary wonder known as another human being?

Lorelei

Every time I walk into a singles bar, I hear Mom's voice, "Don't pick that up—you don't know where it's been."

# *17*

"I'D LIKE TO PROPOSE a toast."

Vivien held up her glass of champagne and the noise level dropped around the dinner table as their guests raised their glasses. "To my roomie, Lauren, for achieving her dream of writing for *Left Coast*. May this be just the beginning."

"Hear, hear!" Robert Li, Viv's dad, grinned at Lauren as he toasted her, while beside him, his mother Ming-mei smiled with the calm grace of a woman sure of her place at the head of the family. Across from Viv, Joanie knocked her champagne back a little faster than was socially acceptable, but Lauren could hardly blame her. This was the first time she'd met the people Viv loved, and Viv's fear of what her grandmother would think of their relationship was a dark thread of anxiety under the celebration.

Lauren stood in her turn and lifted her glass in Josh's direction. "To my partner in crime. Don't forget, Josh was responsible for half that article."

Moments of complete happiness had come at such rare intervals in her life that Lauren could remember each one with complete clarity. A trip to San Gregorio Beach alone with her dad when she was six, clouded by his subsequent departure. The night of the fireworks on the roof with her foster family. The dean of the Berkeley School of Journalism handing her that diploma. Helping Rory throw a party for Mikki and Nolan after they'd eloped. And finally, the phone call from John Garvey at *Left Coast* to tell her they were accepting the cybersex article and offering her an astonishing sum for her half of it.

She knew *Left Coast* paid its contributors well, but she hadn't expected it to be *that* well. No wonder the competition was so fierce and the magazine's standards so high. Even seeing the article's headline on the magazine's glossy cover in every newsstand in town last Tuesday hadn't measured up to the sheer elation of that phone call.

She drained her glass and Josh got up to open another bottle. Normally she and Viv didn't serve Veuve Clicquot at their table. On the contrary; whatever was on sale at BevMo was usually good enough for them. But Josh had brought the champagne and, being women of both practicality and taste, they had hustled the bottles into the fridge without a word of argument.

Life was good. Damn good.

If only Viv could come out to her grandma and be able to openly show her affection for Joanie, life would be perfect. As it was, Joanie had been introduced as a co-worker of Josh's, and so far Ming-mei hadn't noticed the desperate, longing game of footsie that was going on at the far end of the table. Despite the celebration going on all around her, Joanie looked on the point of tears and Vivien was faking vivacity with all the grit she could muster.

She and Joanie had thrown themselves into preparation for the meal. Lauren had wondered whether they thought that if they showed Ming-mei they were excellent cooks and perfect hostesses, it would smooth the way a little. But Lauren didn't see how it could. Ming-mei had her expectations about Viv's future and those included a suitable husband and a family, neither of which interested Viv in the least.

"I don't see what the fuss is about," Emma had said one night a couple of years ago. Lauren had dropped over shortly after Viv had broken the news to her dad that he wouldn't need to save his money for a wedding dress, two changes of gowns, and a cheongsam at a massive wedding reception. "She's living on her own, working and living a perfectly normal life. What business is it of her grandmother's if she wants a female partner?"

"She loves her grandma," Lauren had tried to explain.

"Well, you love me, too, but I hope that doesn't mean you wouldn't come and tell me anything you wanted. If you decided you were in love with a woman, I'd be nothing but happy for you. Love isn't something to get angry about, Romeo and Juliet notwithstanding."

"But you're a child of the sixties. Ming-mei was born in China and the expectations are that daughters marry and have kids. She's a strong personality and Viv, much as I love her, cares more about never being spoken to again than she does for her own happiness."

Emma had not been able to understand a grown woman of twenty-five who would allow someone to hold her happiness hostage to their expectations. In Emma's view, until Viv learned that she had to go after her heart's desire, she wasn't going to get it, and that was that.

To catch a few minutes together, Viv and Joanie loaded the dishwasher while Lauren cut one of Rory's mouthwatering cheesecakes. Her sister baked bread for a living, but for entertainment she could be sweet-talked into making other things. She named her cheesecakes after movies, and this one happened to be *La Dolce Vita* and involved dollops of caramel hidden inside what looked like an innocent plain cake.

Next to chocolate truffles and Josh and selling magazine articles, caramel was pretty much Lauren's favorite thing in the world.

Robert Li had to be up early for a business trip the next day—something to do with a holdup in a silicon chip's design in Singapore—so he and Ming-mei left shortly after nine.

"*Xie-xie* for a lovely dinner," Ming-mei said, hugging Lauren at the door.

"I didn't have anything to do with it," she protested, smiling. "Vivien and Joanie made everything, and my sister contributed dessert."

"But your success gave us the occasion."

"Mrs. Li, Vivien worked hard to make sure everything was perfect. You should give her credit."

"She pulled the skins of the *shui jao* too tight so they broke in the boiling water. In Shandong province we are famous for our dumplings. No woman in my family would serve dumplings with holes in them. She spent too much time giggling with that Lam girl."

Lauren's heart sank. "Well, don't forget Viv has never been to Shandong province, and I thought the dumplings were great. I love having Joanie around. She makes me laugh, too."

But Ming-mei wasn't about to be convinced. "I think you're a better friend to my granddaughter. When she's with you, she doesn't ruin the food she serves to her guests."

From the tiny balcony that added another hundred

bucks to the rent, Lauren watched Robert Li and his mother walk to the BART station. Ming-mei moved with grace, every step chosen deliberately, as though she were mapping out Tai Chi moves on the sidewalk.

Lauren realized afresh just why Vivien was so afraid of her disapproval. Li Ming-mei was formidable. What granddaughter wouldn't want such a woman to love her instead of disown her?

A pair of strong arms slipped around her from behind. "I'm going to head out, too," Josh said. "Coming with me?"

Lauren wasn't sure if Joanie was going to stay or not, but the combination of tension and elation had wrung her out. The thought of going back to Josh's cool bed and making love until midnight was unbelievably tempting.

But sometimes loyalty to your friends came before what you wanted yourself.

"I think I'll stay." She leaned back and rubbed her cheek on the shoulder of his jacket, like a contented cat. "Viv is really upset. I'd like to be around if she wants to talk."

"What's she upset about?"

Lauren couldn't betray her friend's confidence. And there was Joanie to consider, too. Everyone at *Left Coast* didn't need to know the details of her romantic life.

"Family stuff," she said vaguely. "You know how it is."

"Don't I." His tone was wry. "What about tomorrow? It's Friday—I could probably sneak off for a long lunch and not come back."

After listening to the Queen of Pain rant for half an hour during their conference call the other week, Lauren was being more conscientious about work. It would take her all morning to catch Lorelei up on what had been going on in the virtual 'hood, and on top of that she wanted to take some of the CyberCon material and work it into a column for *Inside Out*.

"I have to work in the morning, too," she said, "but I can meet you at your place around two."

He kissed her, his breath feathering the skin just below her ear. She felt the longing in his body in the way his hipbones pressed against her derriere and his mouth lingered.

"I'll see you then." He released her reluctantly and went to get his jacket.

"Take the last bottle of champagne with you," she reminded him. He'd laid out the money for it, so he may as well enjoy it.

"No, you keep it. You might need it later."

Truer words were never spoken.

She'd half expected Viv and Joanie to disappear and try to salvage a little joy from the evening. But instead, Joanie gave Viv a fierce hug, whispered, "Good luck," and slipped out the door.

Good luck?

Wow, maybe Viv had reached the end of her tether and was going to go beard her grandmother in her den. If so, it was a darn good thing Josh had left the champagne. They'd need it either before or aft—

"Lauren, can we talk?"

Definitely before. Lauren went into the kitchen, which was so spotless it showed no evidence they'd just thrown a dinner party. The dishwasher churned away under the counter. She found the cork remover in the junk drawer.

"Sure. Just let me open this last bottle of champagne."

"I'd rather you didn't. Come over here and sit down."

Wow again. She was going to go into it cold. Viv had more nerve than she did. Well, if a pep talk was what she needed before she followed her grandma home, Lauren was her girl.

She sat next to her oldest friend and plumped up a pillow made from scraps of her royal-blue Thai silk dress. "Okay. Tell me what's going down."

Viv hesitated, and Lauren made herself a little more comfortable.

"Well...Joanie and I have been talking, and we both concluded there was no other practical way around this. Just let me say in advance that I'm really, really sorry. But, amazing though it seems after such a short time, I think she's The One. I wouldn't do this unless it were that important."

"You're finally going to tell her?" Lauren prompted gently when Vivien paused.

"Tell who what?"

"Your grandma." When Vivien looked at her blankly, she went on, "About you and Joanie."

Viv rolled her beautiful dark eyes. "Oh, yes, I'll have to tell her. But I'm going to ease her into it gently, you see. She loves you, so I thought if she saw Joanie and me living together the way you and I do, she'd get used to her. In advance, sort of."

Lauren focused on the important words. "Living together?"

"Yes. That's what I wanted to talk to you about. We think the best way to do this is for her to move in."

"Here?"

"Yes."

"But this place isn't big enough for three, honey. The bedrooms barely fit a single bed, never mind a queen. Besides, much as I like her, I'm not sure I could handle the heat around here with the two of you." She smiled, but Viv didn't smile back.

She bit her lip instead and inhaled a shaky breath. "You're not hearing me, Lauren. If Joanie moved in, that would mean you would need to move out. She'd have your room. There would just be the two of us."

Lauren stared at her. "You want me to move out?"

"Not want you to. Need you to. I know it's a shock, but now you have Josh, so that's a possibility, or you can always hang at your mom's or one of your sisters' for a while until you find a new place."

"I'm not going to find a rent-controlled place like this one." Viv was silent, and even in the midst of her shock and dismay, Lauren found a grain of relief that she hadn't stated the obvious: that the apartment was in Viv's name because Robert Li had co-signed the lease. Otherwise they'd never have been able to get it, fresh out of college and with nary a dime to their names.

Most of the time she never gave it a thought.

She was giving it one now.

"How can you do this to me after all this time?" Lauren wasn't sure whether to shout or cry.

"I'm so sorry." Viv's eyes swam with tears. "But I don't know what else to do."

"You could just march over there and tell her. You don't have to rearrange your whole life to be beautiful like some kind of tea garden before you do it."

"That's a Japanese philosophy. I'm not Japanese."

"You know what I mean!"

Lauren slouched against the cushions, options scattering in her head like a flock of frightened pigeons. Then one thing became clear.

This was her best friend. This was Viv, who cooked in the middle of the night for her every time she got dumped. With whom she'd been to hell and back during that awful year before Viv came out. Who was responsible, loving, funny and who—dammit all—would make Joanie a fine partner.

Lauren sighed. Who was she to stand in the way of somebody else's happiness the way she'd just accused Ming-mei of doing?

Viv was looking at her as if she expected her to grab a pillow and smother her with it.

"Honey, I'm sorry I upset you." Lauren leaned over and hugged her. "If you think Joanie is The One, then she's a lucky woman."

Viv burst into tears and fell into her arms, snuffling into the side of her neck like a little kid. Lauren patted her back, then looked around a little wildly for anything resembling a tissue.

Paper towel in the kitchen. Good enough.

Lauren got up long enough to fetch one, and when Viv had blown her nose and mopped up her face, she gave her a watery smile. "You have every right to be mad at me."

"I'll leave that up to your grandma. I just need to go over my options, that's all."

Viv blew her nose again. "Don't remind me. Even if this doesn't work, I've made up my mind to tell her when I graduate at the end of next month. By then Joanie and I will be together and it won't matter so much that *nai-nai* hates me and will never speak to me again."

"She's old school, sweetie. But you're her only grandchild. I can't imagine her disowning you because of who you live with."

"I can," Viv sighed.

"Well, if you and Joanie decide to commit, you could

always adopt a little girl from China. I bet that'd bring her around. Who could resist dimples and big brown eyes?"

She'd been teasing, but the look Viv shot her held surprise and revelation. "If she were from Shandong province I bet she couldn't." Then she shook her head and took another swipe at her face with the damp paper towel. "What am I saying? I need to get through graduation first. And live with Joanie for five minutes before I start thinking about heavy-duty adult stuff."

"And I guess I'd better think about packing." Lauren looked around at the shabby but cheerful little place she'd called home for nearly six years. "The first of July will be here before you know it."

And then what?

Unbidden, the image of the cool sanctuary Josh called home floated in front of her mind's eye like a mirage. Not Pacific Heights, but it may as well be. Roomy. With the scent of his cologne in the closet. For a moment she indulged in sheer fantasy. She could set up her home office in his spare room instead of making do with a corner of the kitchen counter.

She'd have to tell him about Lorelei, but now that she'd proven to *Left Coast* that she was their kind of writer, that shouldn't be a problem. He knew who she really was and that Lorelei was just a fiction that kept *Inside Out* squarely in the public eye. Sometimes spitting in it, but there you were. What had John Garvey said? That Lorelei had a talent for getting people to talk.

*Change,* a voice in her head said softly. *Maybe this is the start of something big.*

# *18*

IN TIMES OF TROUBLE, Lauren did what generations of smart, independent women before her had done.

She went home to Mom.

"This is only for a couple of weeks," she assured Emma for probably the fourth time as she struggled up the stairs with the last of her cardboard boxes. "As soon as I find a place, I'll be out of here."

Emma leaned on the doorjamb of Mikki's old room, which Lauren was using for temporary storage. There was not much left of her vivacious, strong-willed sister except for the Nine Inch Nails logo decoupaged to the back of the closet door and the eggplant walls from her purple phase.

"Stay as long as you like. Fortunately, Arun found his own place last weekend and moved out. Are you sure this is it?"

Lauren surveyed her boxes. Her clothes were already hung in the closet of her old room, and there was a desk in here where she could set up her laptop to work. The eggplant color was surprisingly soothing, though she hadn't thought so at the time. Probably her opinions had been colored by Mikki's stubborn insistence on getting her own way. That was one of the things that had been hard to love about her sister, but it sure served the kids well in the foster care system now.

"It doesn't look like much for six years of independent living, does it?"

"You aren't a pack rat like some of us."

"I wouldn't call you a pack rat, Mom. We're not wading through alleys of newspapers from 1983, are we?"

Emma laughed. "There are degrees of pack rat-ness. I just haven't advanced to the later stages. I have plenty of stuff from 1983. And 1973. And 1963, for that matter."

"Funny how most of the stuff you save turns out to be collectors' items and first editions."

"Sweetie, anything can be a collector's item. Look at your César dress."

"Dresses. I got another one not long ago. The girl who gave it to me paid five bucks for it at a thrift shop. Can you believe it?" Thank goodness Josh had rescued it after she'd had her meltdown at CyberCon and had given it back to her.

"See?" Emma said. "You'd be surprised what people think is junk—until somebody else wants it."

"Speaking of wanting what other people have, do you know a guy named James McCrae?"

Emma pushed herself from the doorjamb and led the way down to the kitchen. "Sure do. Any relation to Josh?"

"His dad." Emma made a noise in her throat that could mean anything. "I hear you have something he wants."

"Me and everyone else on this block. The man is unbelievably arrogant and short-sighted." She pulled a pitcher out of the fridge. "But then, he thinks I'm not only stubborn, but fat to boot."

"He told you that you were fat?" Lauren was aghast.

"That bastard. I should have upended the gravy boat on his head while I had the chance. You are *not* fat. He could have asked any one of your legion of lovers."

"That may have been part of the problem."

"Your lovers? How did *that* come up?"

"Do you want some of this? It's raspberry smoothie."

"Yogurt or ice cream?"

"Yogurt, of course. Homemade. This isn't Baskin-Robbins."

"I'd love some. But you didn't answer my question. Why should James McCrae care about how many men fall at your feet and adore you?"

Emma poured Lauren a tall glass and handed it to her. "It might bug him if, deep down, he wanted to join them."

Halfway through a frothy, cool swallow, Lauren coughed and set the glass on the counter with a clank. "Oh, my God. The Emma mojo strikes again."

"Oh, I have no proof." Emma waved a hand, then took a sip of her drink. "Just a feeling. I've seen that look often enough. You know, that 'does she or doesn't she' look."

"Ewwwww."

"Don't give me 'ew.' You girls and your 'mojo,' as if I have no agency in the matter. You know I still have a healthy sexual appetite."

"Not 'ew' you, 'ew' him. He was probably looking at you the way Bill Gates looks at Netscape."

"Something like," Emma agreed. "How's your smoothie?"

"Like a little bit of heaven." She took another mouthful, a little slower this time. "No wonder he got so angry at the dinner table. Called you names and everything. But the really fun part was when Josh stood up to him and Irene made him apologize to me."

"Did they? Good for them."

"Now he hates both of us. May as well keep it in the family."

"What if it affects your relationship with Josh?"

"It already has." Emma waited, and Lauren shot her a grin around the rim of her glass. "We had oral sex on the third-floor staircase twenty minutes later."

Emma burst into laughter. "I knew there was a reason I liked that boy." Then she asked, "Does he know you and Vivien aren't sharing the apartment anymore?"

"Oh, yeah. He took a carload of old clothes to the homeless shelter for us."

"But you're still here."

Lauren began to understand her mother's drift. "No, he didn't invite me to move in while he was at it."

"Do you want him to?"

She finished her smoothie and turned to the sink to rinse the glass, then put it in the dishwasher. "It was a nice little fantasy while it lasted. But it's too soon to be thinking about it. It hasn't even been two months."

"Quality beats quantity, I always thought."

"True, but not everybody thinks the way you do."

"What do *you* want, Lauren-my-love?"

Lauren smiled at the affectionate nickname. Good question. Hard answer. "I want him."

"Does he know that?"

"If the third-floor staircase was any indication, I'd say yes."

"There's more to it than sex if you're going to share living space. Remember Ahmad." She pronounced his name *Ach-mahd,* and followed it with a dreamy sigh.

"The one who proposed, then went away in a huff when you said yes, if you could keep separate houses?"

"The very same." Emma's eyes were bright with

memory. "How I loved that man. Such good company, and as for the bedroom—" she fanned herself "—whew! But my God, he was impossible to live with. Never picked up a single thing he dropped, and his taste in music included everything—as long as the windows vibrated in time with it."

"I can't believe he let you go over a silly thing like logistics."

"I know," her mother admitted. "Men are strange creatures." She finished off her drink. "Well, I hope you two work it out. Despite having an unfortunate father, Josh seems to make you happy, and I'm all for that. So, now that you're home—" Emma waggled hopeful eyebrows "—do you remember what box your DVD collection is in?"

JOSH WAS UNDER NO obligation to invite her to live with him.

Lauren snuggled under the Victorian crazy quilt she'd pieced when she was sixteen and tried to let the familiar smell of old wood, fresh cotton and the scent of the spray of freesia that Emma had left in a bud vase on her nightstand soothe her into sleep.

The fact that he had not, worried her.

Oh, sure, she was going to get her own place. She could support herself and live as independently as Mikki and Rory did, but that wasn't the point. She probably wouldn't move in anyway, even if he had asked her.

She hadn't been saying brave things for her mother's benefit a couple of days ago, she'd meant it. It was too soon. The relationship she had with Josh was in the fun new stage where they did things together and made knee-melting love and talked on the phone a couple of times a day. Who wanted to mess with that by moving in together and facing the prosaic realities of dirty socks and closet space and what to do with the second toaster?

Not that she owned a toaster—the one in their apartment had been Viv's—but still.

He might have asked, though. Then she would have turned him down and they'd go back to normal, but with a subtle difference. She would have known that he wanted something a little more permanent. She didn't have to want it, but it would have been nice to know that he did.

*You are such a liar.*

*Why? I like being independent. I'm focusing on my career. I'm crazy about Josh, but I'm not ready to live with him yet.*

*Liar, liar, pants on fire.*

*Okay. Fine. So maybe I'd give it some serious consideration if he did ask me. But he didn't, so that's that.*

*Go and talk to him about it.*

*What, and give him a reason to run? You heard him. He's already jumped a few of the usual hurdles for me. I don't want to throw up a big one and watch him bobble at it.*

*Don't you trust him? Don't you trust what's between you?*

*Of course I do. It's just new, that's all.*

*New has nothing to do with it. If you trust the man, go talk to him. At least let him know how you feel.*

*Honesty is always good, that's true. And I'm going to see him tomorrow night.*

*If you can write an article about cybersex together, you can talk about your own relationship.*

*Good point. Then maybe we can stop writing and talking and just get down to doing.*

*That's more like it.*

AT 11:06 ON THURSDAY morning, Vivien called.

"Hey, sweetie, how's it going?" Lauren uploaded a blog entry for Lorelei with one hand while she held her cell phone in the other. "Thanks for the message about my bathing suit, by the way. I have no idea how it got that far back in the closet. Maybe it crawled away in humiliation. I think I wrote it off and got a new one."

"Lauren, do you have a minute?"

Uh-oh. That didn't sound good. "Is everything okay between you and Joanie?"

"Oh, sure. We decided to turn your room into a shared office and clothes space and both use mine."

"Even though it means you have to take a running leap from the door to get into bed?"

"Going to bed was pretty interesting before. This just makes it fun. The original Chinese acrobats, that's us."

Smiling, Lauren pushed away from her laptop and propped her feet on the desk in Mikki's old room. "So, what's up?"

"Well, BrasCo is going through another funding cycle for this little software company that makes a game called *Contact,* so that means a bunch of paperwork. And being the Princess of Paperwork, it falls to me to file it."

*Contact?* A vision wearing a red tank top danced across the monitor of Lauren's memory. "I thought you were the receptionist."

"My duties were, um, expanded."

"You mean, they laid off the file clerk."

"Something like that. So now I have one of those nifty remote phones you hook on your belt and I can spend all day in the file room and deal with the switch at the same time."

"Vivien, that is sick. That's practically slave labor."

"Grad school lasts for two years, but student loans are with us forever. So, do you want to know about the phone system or about what I found out in the filing?"

"Oh, definitely the filing. This sounds like groundbreaking news, here." Why on earth would Viv think that beautiful Maddie's funding would matter to her? Was some kind of corporate scandal about to break?

"It was to me," Viv replied. "You probably already know all about it, but I had no idea. I thought the guy was just a journalist."

What guy? "Viv, start at the beginning. What journalist?"

"Your journalist. Josh. I had no idea he owned a third of *Left Coast*. I thought he just wrote for them. No wonder his picture is so nice."

"What?" The word came out in a whisper, which was all Lauren could manage. She felt as if someone had sucker-punched her.

"Oh, you didn't know. Well, hey, Nancy Drew comes through again."

Lauren tried to get something sensible out of her mouth, but nothing happened.

"Lauren? Are you there?"

"I'm here." He *owned* part of the magazine. Owned it and had never said a word. Had let her think he was just a freelancer like herself.

Well, gee, Lauren, no wonder your article was accepted. John Garvey isn't likely to turn down the guy who votes on his salary, now, is he?

"Who'd've thought the guy was a venture capitalist? Except for his yummy car he seemed pretty normal. According to this paperwork, he funded *Contact* first, and BrasCo is doing their second cycle. I did some checking in the stock database and it looks like he bought into the magazine when it started up five years ago. Sorry if I'm being nosy, but it was interesting, since I know the guy and all." Viv paused. "Lauren, are you sure you're there?"

"Viv, I've got to go."

"Are you okay?"

"Yeah, I'm fine. Thanks for the call. I'll talk to you later."

She turned off the phone with hands that didn't really seem connected to her body. Then she snatched her purse off the bed.

"Lauren?" Emma called as she raced past the kitchen. "I'm making lunch. Do you want some?"

The slam of the front door was her only answer.

JOSH GLANCED AT CALLER I.D. and resisted the urge to bang his head on his keyboard. Instead, he pressed the button on the speakerphone with what he figured was commendable restraint.

"What is it this time, Jillian?"

After he'd shown up at the Black on White Ball with Lauren on his arm, Jillian hadn't backed off the way he'd expected. Instead, her sideways attentions had become even more frequent, to the point where he could count on at least one irrelevant question per lunch hour, and often two or three.

"Lauren Massey to see you." Her brevity communicated the depth of her dislike.

"Send her in. Thanks, Jillian."

Click.

Feeling as if his day had brightened about two hundred percent, Josh headed in the direction of reception and met Lauren halfway.

"Are you all right?" She was pale, not just because

she had no makeup on, but because her skin was the color of paper. Two scarlet spots burned under her cheekbones.

"I'm fine. I am not here because of me."

Huh? "Come on back."

"Is a conference room free?"

He glanced at her over his shoulder as they wound through the maze of cubes. "Is this a business meeting? Did I mess up the calendar? It happens sometimes, when I don't sync up my PDA with the—"

"I would have thought you'd have your own office. A corner one, at that." Her tone was brittle as she surveyed the real estate.

He showed her into the smallest of the conference rooms. She was upset about something, that was for sure. It had to be work related. If it were personal she would have waited until tonight, when they were supposed to have dinner.

"I have no idea what that means," he said. He pulled out a chair, but she ignored him and went to stand by the window. With a mental shrug, he hitched a hip onto the conference room table and waited.

"I didn't think *Left Coast* was a cheapskate operation, but maybe it is if they house one of their principal investors in a lousy cube."

Oh. Damn. He should have told her himself. *Josh, you idiot.* "How did you find out?"

"I'm a *real* journalist, Josh," she snapped. "I have sources. When were you planning to tell me you own thirty percent of this magazine?"

"Thirty-three. And as for telling you, I was going to, but I didn't think it was relevant. To us, I mean."

"Not relevant?" Her voice escalated to a squeak and she took a deep breath to calm herself. "You don't think it's relevant that you own the magazine that (a) offered me a spec job on the condition that I work with you and (b) bought the work after I (c) fricking slept with you? How in the hell do you think that makes me feel?"

No wonder she'd suggested the conference room. As it was, her voice was probably carrying to half the offices through the ventilation system.

"That's not how it was, Lauren."

"Tell me how it was. Or better yet, let me tell you. *Left Coast* gave me this story because of you, and they bought it because of you. Not because of me. Not because it was good. But because one of their investors co-wrote it and it would be political suicide to turn him down."

"Not true."

"Did. You. Get. Me. That. Job?"

Muscles flexed in her jaw. He could gloss over the truth to make her feel better, but she deserved more than that.

"I recommended you. Your experience and talent got you the job."

"Did they buy it because of you?"

"No."

"You seriously expect me to believe they wouldn't print an article written by one of their funding principals?"

"Not if it was crap. And it wasn't crap. It was good. We're getting tons of mail about it."

"Were you even thinking about telling me what you really do for a living?"

How was he supposed to answer that? "Yes, I had thought about it. But I don't make my living as a venture capitalist anymore. That's like an old life. It crops up now and again, like with meeting Maddie Matsumoto at the convention, but the truth is, journalism is what I've always wanted to do. It's what's important to me now. And you know all about that."

"You don't think it would matter to me that you weren't honest about it?"

"Would it have made you turn down the work?"

"It certainly would have! All I need is for everyone to think I got my story published because I slept with you. My professional rep would be shot to crap. It probably already is."

"No one here knows about my stake in the magazine except Tina Bianchi and John."

"Bull."

"And maybe the people whose offices share this room's ventilation system."

Never try to be funny with a woman in a temper.

"I'm sorry, Josh. I just can't get past this. This is the second time you've done something like this to me. If there's anything I need from a man, it's trust and honesty. Not job handouts. Or the wrong kind of professional exposure." She walked to the door and gave him a long look that was equal parts sadness and anger, with a little betrayal mixed in. "I'd say see you around, but I probably won't. I'll cancel the reservations for tonight."

Cancel? Goodbye? What? "Goodbye as in now or goodbye as in permanently?"

Her beautiful lips, that he'd kissed so recently and fantasized about this very morning in staff meeting, twisted. "You figure it out."

And then she walked out the door and out of his life.

# 19

JOSH STOOD OUT ON THE FRONT porch of the Edwardian stick on Garrison Street and tried to calculate the amount of money there must be in the neighborhood's renovation pool to produce upkeep as beautiful as this. It wasn't in a high-income area, the hill was steep and there was an auto repair shop at the end of the block, but it was obvious a lot of thought had gone into paint, trims and embellishments like the lacy gingerbread on the house next door.

Or a lot of love, if you believed Lauren, which his dad did not. *Mrs. Delaney came to that house as a bride in 1948...*

The door opened and he turned to see a tall woman with wise eyes and graying reddish hair, wearing bifocals and an Oriental-looking padded jacket the same color as the dress Lauren had worn to Sunday night dinner. She cradled a mug of pink tea.

"Mrs. Constable?"

"Emma. Nice to meet you at last, Josh." He must have looked a little surprised, because she smiled. "I read *Left Coast*."

Oh. The head shot. Right.

Uh-oh. She'd have read the article, too. But now was not the time to think about that.

"And if Lauren made it through a single conversation in the last two months without mentioning your name, I missed it," she added. "Please come in."

He followed her into a sitting room next to the front door, overlooking the street. Two women lounged on the couch, one whom he recognized as Aurora Constable holding another mug of pink tea and the brunette from Lauren's photograph holding an enormous paper cup with a popular coffee bar's label on the front. The brunette gave him a laser look of challenge with striking blue eyes that didn't miss a thing.

Lauren's sisters. Of all mornings to show up unannounced, this one had to be the worst from a survival point of view.

Through an open archway in the rear, he saw a kitchen and dining room, with a great big...thing hanging from the beam. It looked as if Shelob the spider from the *Lord of the Rings* had gone insane with brown twine.

"Can I offer you some Red Zinger?" Emma asked. "I just made a fresh pot."

"No. But thank you."

"Have you met Lauren's sisters? Aurora Constable and Michaela Correlli."

"Rory," the baker said as he shook hands.

"You can stick with Michaela for now," the brunette said. He tried not to wince at her tone.

He took a seat on a bench partly covered in books that stood in front of the empty fireplace. "That's quite a...sculpture you have hanging there." He hoped she hadn't paid actual money for it.

"Thanks." Emma sat in an armchair across from her daughters, folding her legs under her like a girl. "Mountain Girl made it for me one year. Jerry's wife," she said by way of explanation when he looked blank. "Road trips last forever so most of us took up some kind of handwork. It was either that or hallucinogens." She laughed, gazing at the…thing affectionately. "Are you a Dead fan?"

Mountain Girl…Jerry…road trips…

"Jerry Garcia? *Jerry Garcia's* wife made that for you?"

She nodded serenely. "After this she lost interest in macramé and went onto something else. Needlepoint, I think."

"It's a collector's item," Michaela said from behind her coffee. "She's been offered thousands for it."

The gazes of all three women settled on him and in the companionable silence among them, he felt the unspoken urge to spit out what he'd come for. "I'm hoping Lauren is home and that I can see her."

Emma shook her head. "I'm afraid she isn't."

"She's staying with Rory for a day or two." Was it his imagination or did Michaela's tone have an "I dare you to go and get her" ring to it? He'd never met her before, yet he got the definite impression she didn't like him.

"Can you give me a phone number? I've left messages on her cell phone but she isn't returning them. So far," he added, as a point of pride.

"I don't think so," Michaela said, dismissing him. She took a sip of coffee.

That should have made him angry. He should have been getting fired up with the challenge of extracting information out of this wall of women. But instead, his pride whistled out of him like air from a deflating tire. "I wish I knew how to fix this," he said to the carpet.

"She feels betrayed," Emma said gently, and blew on her tea. "I'm sure you understand that."

"Since you betrayed her," Rory said, clearly meaning to clarify the situation.

"I don't see how this whole thing is a betraying kind of offense." He felt goaded past the point of politeness. "It's just a job. And an old one at that."

He realized he sounded hurt, but there wasn't a damn thing he could do about it. Make a plan, give it your best shot, win. That strategy had served him well in both journalism and venture capital. He just wasn't used to failure. It frustrated him, made him look even harder for the fix.

Only, in this situation there didn't seem to be one.

"I don't think it's the old job as much as it is the fact that you kept it back from her when it was important to her career," Emma pointed out.

"Her career would be just fine whether she knows I hold part of the magazine or not."

"Her sense of ethics is obviously stronger than yours," Michaela observed.

"Ease up, Mikki." Rory nudged her with an elbow, then looked at Josh. "Try to see this from her point of view. You're in a sexual relationship, right?"

"Uh…" He glanced at Emma, who laughed.

"Don't look at me like that. I was having sex before you were born."

"Okay, so you're in this relationship, having sex, which in case you haven't noticed, women take fairly seriously. Lauren certainly does. She expects a certain amount of sharing to come with that intimacy. And what you each do for a living is one of the first things people typically share."

"So why'd you keep it from her?" Michaela wanted to know.

*Nobody expects the Spanish Inquisition.* "I told you,

I didn't think it was important. Writing means more to me now than the venture capitalist stuff. I did what I needed to do in business and now I'm moving on to something more rewarding. That includes journalism and Lauren."

"Not in that order, I take it."

Josh glared at Michaela. "Are you always this combative with Lauren's boyfriends?"

She glared back. "Only when they make my sister cry."

"She cried?" He sat back on the bench. "Tell me I didn't make her cry."

"Did she cry?" Michaela appealed to Rory.

"She did." Rory nodded. "Therefore, you won't be calling her. Or following me home to talk to her. Or doing whatever else you were thinking of doing. If she wants to contact you, she knows your number."

"Unless, of course, there's something you want one of us to pass on to her. I'm willing to take a message."

Josh had a feeling that trusting Michaela over this would be like trusting a cat not to jump a bird. It was easy to imagine what she'd do with any kind of message, up to and including twisting it so it would sound as though he never wanted to see Lauren again.

"I guess I was being selfish," he said at last. "I should have told her. God knows I would have felt the same way in her position."

"How much does she mean to you?" Emma's eyes were sincere and Josh felt a glimmer of hope. Maybe there was a chink in the wall. Well, if they wanted honesty, they'd get honesty.

"Everything," he said simply. "Sometimes I act as though life is a one-way street and it's all going my way. But I've structured things to be that way because it's safe. Dull sometimes, but achievable and safe."

He remembered the picnic on the beach and smiled. "Lauren makes me turn corners. Stop at lights and then run them. Hell, sometimes she makes me run off the road altogether and then laugh about it." He held Emma's gaze. "My key may have fit her lock at that party where we met, but she fits me in a way I only learned to appreciate when I couldn't be with her anymore." He took a breath and then said quietly, "I hope you understand. Tell her that, if nothing else."

Silence filled the room again, until Michaela's voice broke it. "That's the most beautiful thing I've ever heard."

This time Rory's elbow had a little more force behind it. "Give him a break. I think he means it."

"They all think they do," Michaela sighed.

Josh spared a moment to wonder who had done the mambo in cleated boots on *her* heart.

"I'll pass on your message, Josh," Rory said gently.

He flashed her a grateful smile, putting everything he had into it. Her eyes widened and she blinked.

He got up. "Thank you. Tell Lauren—" He stopped himself. *Never drag out the ending.* "Never mind. I'll let myself out."

He glanced into the room as he pulled the door shut behind him. All three of the women who loved Lauren the most were watching him.

And no one smiled.

"DID YOU HEAR? Did you hear what he said?"

Mikki and Rory pounded up the stairs. Lauren straightened from her cramped position over the ornate metal heating grate in her room—the one that opened directly over the living room.

She sat on her bed as both Mikki and Rory stampeded through the door like a pair of teenagers and threw themselves next to her on the crazy quilt.

"Oh, my God, Rory, she's crying."

Rory dashed into the bathroom and came back with a few squares of toilet paper. "Here."

Lauren blew her nose and scrubbed the dry part over her cheeks. "I can't believe he said that. He really cares."

"The question you have to ask yourself is, do you?"

"Mikki, for Pete's sake, she wouldn't be crying if she didn't care," Rory said impatiently. "I'm beginning to care myself. Did you see that smile? And the dimples? And the eyes?"

"Don't you dare!" Lauren's tears dried up as she glared at her sister.

"Hell, no." Rory waved her off. "I have enough on my plate with Tuck. But my, my, you can bring those dimples into the family gene pool with my blessing."

"Yes, he has great eyes. And the dimples are good, too. But I am not ready to think about the gene pool," Lauren said with dignity, and tossed the wadded-up tissue into the trash. "I need to think about a graceful way to back down without him thinking I came running the minute he wanted me to."

"I can't believe he just came right out and said that to us," Mikki said. "We're perfect strangers to him."

"It wasn't like you did anything to make him feel warm and fuzzy," Rory reminded her. "You are so harsh."

"You can't make it too easy for them, otherwise they get cocky."

"Right. That's working so well with Nolan." Mikki's gaze dropped to her hands and Rory hugged her repentantly. "I'm sorry. That was a shitty thing to say."

Mikki hugged her back, wordlessly accepting the apology. "We'll blame it on Tuck. He has broad shoulders. So, Lauren, what are you going to do?"

Lauren punched up a pillow behind her back and settled in for a serious strategy session. "I have a couple of options. I could go hop on the train and follow him over to his place and have terrific make-up sex."

"Sounds good," Mikki allowed, nodding.

"Or I could return one of his many messages, arrange to meet for dinner, then drive to his place with him in his Porsche and have terrific make-up sex."

"Also good," Rory agreed. "But you're forgetting one thing."

"I am?"

"We're talking make-up sex here," Mikki interrupted. "What else is there?"

"Lauren's Lies." Rory raised her eyebrows.

Of course. If she and Josh were going to get anywhere, she was going to have to come clean, too. And that meant telling him who was really behind "Lorelei on the Loose."

"It'll be okay now," Mikki said. "Didn't you hear the guy? He can't live without you. What harm can Lorelei do when the guy comes right out and says this to your family? It's practically like asking for your hand."

"Under that prickly exterior, Michaela Correlli, you are such a romantic," Lauren told her, smiling with affection.

"I said *practically*. I think you have a little work yet."

"I do." Lauren thought for a moment. "He reads Lorelei every morning. So, if you'll excuse me, I have some writing to do."

*From Lorelei's blog*

I have a confession to make.

Normally I don't read *Left Coast* magazine, that high-toned and fancy publication that wouldn't hire a mere blogger like me on the principle that it would get its metaphorical fingers dirty. However, an informant on this very board told me that if I were interested in even more fame than I currently enjoy, there was something about me in the May 16 issue.

Naturally I headed for the nearest doctor's office at a dead run. Well, you don't think I'd pay to read it, do you?

But there I was, on page 129, in an article written by the bootylicious Josh McCrae, who can track mud into my chatroom anytime. But where? you ask. I don't see your name anywhere. This is where the confession comes in. Are you ready?

I am Lacey, the flash relationship.

A thin disguise, I know. Those of you who are my regulars will have recognized me instantly. So there you have it. Lorelei is guilty of a flash relationship, and may I say, it was divine.

   Mr. Josh McCrae, I got your message. You'll find mine in storage locker 69—appropriate, yes?—at the bus station.

Lorelei

Don't bother me. I'm living happily ever after.

# 20

JOSH'S COFFEE WENT DOWN his throat the wrong way and he coughed and gasped for breath, which was hard to do while staring goggle-eyed at the computer screen.

Lorelei = Lacey. Lacey = Lauren. If A equals B and B equals C, then A must equal C.

"I knew it!" he told the monitor once he'd recovered the ability to speak and breathe. "I *knew* you sounded a little too much like her."

What a kick. He remembered all that bad-mouthing of Lorelei they'd done at the Black on White Ball while she'd sat there as quietly as a list lurker. No wonder she'd stuck it out instead of hightailing it out of there or giving herself away. In the end John Garvey had said out loud that he wanted *Left Coast* to have its own blogger. With an article in the can and the managing editor already thinking in that direction, landing a permanent gig wasn't outside the realm of possibility.

She'd pulled it off so well that they might even get around the stigma of her working for *Inside Out*. If they could persuade Tina Bianchi that Lauren could keep a secret as well as any federal agent—and better than most—a new career as a blogger for *Left Coast* might just become a reality.

But for now he had a gig of his own, so he'd better get moving. Odds were that more than one man—or woman, for that matter—would be racing down to the bus station to grab that message.

But he'd bet most of them didn't own a Porsche Carrera.

Exactly twenty minutes after he'd wiped the coffee off his monitor, Josh strolled into the downtown bus station with the locker key he'd found in an envelope under the Porsche's windshield wiper.

She was doing it again. Not only had she given him the biggest surprise of the year, she was throwing him another loop by turning their reunion into a treasure hunt. Well, he was going to make sure the payoff was worth it. Already his blood was humming with anticipation at what kind of treasure he would find at the end of the rainbow.

A small crowd had gathered around locker 69 and a guy in a charcoal suit was bent to the lock, trying to pick it with a paper clip.

"Excuse me," Josh said loudly, "but I think you have the wrong locker."

"No way, man." The guy straightened, smoothing his tie into place. "I was here first."

"Me second." A guy in dreads held up what was clearly a set of picks.

"But I have the key." Josh flashed it, then folded it into his palm in case anybody got any ideas about tackling him.

"How'd you get that?"

"Look, this is a personal matter between me and the owner of that locker. Would you mind getting out of the way?"

"Hey, aren't you Josh McCrae?"

"Yes."

"You know Lorelei? People have been trying to find out who he is for years."

"He? Lorelei's a woman, and that's all I'm going to say."

"Is this true love?" A teenage girl wanted to know. "Are you guys, like, having an online affair?"

"Is it true you nailed Lorelei?"

"What's she like in bed?"

"Do you enjoy being dominated, Mr. McCrae? Does she wear leather?"

"Dudes." A blond man wearing Jerusalem cruisers and cutoff denims ambled over. "Is this, like, a flash mob? Are you gonna, like, shout a word?"

While half the crowd explained what was going on, Josh shouldered his way through the other half to the locker. They pressed close around him, craning to see what was inside. He inserted the key and turned it. The people at his back took a collective breath as he swung the door open.

*Better move fast.*

He grabbed the white envelope that was all the locker contained, slammed the door and turned to face the crowd. "Okay, folks, game over. Let me through, please."

"Aren't you going to open it?"

"Let us see!"

"This is so romantic."

"No way." He regretted not having gone out for football back in the day. Those skills would be helpful here. "Keep an eye on the boards. Maybe Lorelei will tell you the whole story."

It would be poetic justice if she did, for which he could hardly blame her.

Five minutes later he was back at the car, with only a few scuffs on his shoes where people had trampled his feet. Not bad for his first brush with Lorelei's fans and wannabe lovers.

He slit the envelope and pulled out a sheet of paper. A small silver key exactly like the one that had fit the lock in Lauren's charm the night of the key party fell into his lap.

Nice going, Josh. I hope you didn't have too much competition over the locker. You won't have any at the next one, I promise. The lock that fits this key is at 1411 Jollay. I'll leave the door open for you.

He gunned the Porsche down the hill toward the waterfront wondering what he'd find at that address. With Lauren, it could be anything from an empty lot to a strip club to a hotel. Would she answer the door wearing nothing but cellophane and a smile? Or was the girl in the bus station right, and he'd have to unbuckle a hundred metal rings to get her out of her leather outfit? Or—happy thought—would she simply be in bed wearing a suitcase charm on a necklace and nothing else?

*Come on,* he urged the traffic light at the bottom of the hill. *I'm in a hurry, here.*

Jollay Avenue turned out to be a tiny street in the Marina District, and 1411 was a well-kept row house painted gray with green trim.

It reminded him of the colors on those bakery boxes that Lauren loved to—

Josh turned off the Porsche and pocketed the keys, staring up at the little house as he got out. Of course. He hoped Rory Constable was either not home or had selective hearing, because the reunion he had in mind was not going to be quiet.

The door, which was shiny with new paint, swung open when he turned the handle. He stepped into a cool, dark vestibule. To his right was a living room, to the left a dining room and the biggest kitchen he'd ever seen. A worktable took up most of the space and industrial ovens formed a double stack on one wall.

Definitely Rory's place.

There was no sign of Lauren. He tested the air for a hint of her perfume, but all he breathed in was the scent of recently baked bread. She had to be upstairs. Feeling a little like a cat burglar, Josh took the stairs two at a time and at the landing had another look around.

Empty bedroom with queen-size bed and various crystal bottles on a glass tray on the dresser à la old Hollywood. Spotless, like the rest of the house. Obviously, Rory's room.

The next room was storage. The door of the last room was closed.

Slowly he pushed it open.

Lauren lay on her side on the bed, her head propped on one hand and a book in front of her. She wore a César dress, the purple one the fortune-teller had given her. The little suitcase charm hung at her throat on a silver chain.

Somehow, that seemed more right than cellophane or leather or even blatant nakedness.

"I hope you've got period underwear on under that," he said.

She glanced at the clock on the nightstand. "Exactly one hour and forty-seven minutes from upload to arrival. Damn, you're good."

He crossed the room in one bound and stretched out

next to her on the bed. "I had a clear trail to follow, once I elbowed all the competition out of the way."

"Was there a crowd at the bus station?"

"Yep. It might have been a flash mob, though. By the time I left they were undecided whether to just shout a word and leave or to follow me over here. Diverse bunch of fans you've got. The guy in the dreads with the set of lock picks was the best."

She laughed. "That's David Aristos. He's a cop with the S.F.P.D."

"No way."

"Yup. He sent me his picture once and swore me to secrecy. They're a loyal bunch. Some of them have been with me since the beginning. Probably half of them were there to check you out and make sure your intentions were honorable." She paused. "I should have told you about Lorelei a long time ago. After I was done yelling at you about keeping your thirty-three percent from me."

He ran a slow finger along her jaw, tracing the slender strength in her bone structure, then dropped his finger to the suitcase charm and toyed with it. "Is she the skeleton in your closet the way the stake in the magazine is in mine?"

"Yes, but thirty-three percent of a magazine isn't quite the career killer Lorelei is."

"I wouldn't say that. John Garvey seemed to think he needed someone like her on our Web site."

"It'll never happen, even if you pull rank and lean on him. Tina can't afford to have someone from an activist paper in such a public position."

Maybe. Maybe not. Tina cared about the bottom line and was prepared to forgive a lot for it.

"Lauren?" He leaned his forehead on hers and gazed into those hazel eyes.

"Mmm?"

"Why are we talking business?"

"Because business has been the wrench in our works since the beginning?"

She had a point.

"And because I want everything out on the table now, with no more skeletons in anybody's closet, before I answer your question about my period underwear."

He grinned, a devilish smile that made her eyes widen and put an answering smile in the curve of her lips. "I bet I can get an answer on that score without you saying a word."

"I bet you can, but first, there's something you should know."

"Oh, God." He couldn't imagine what else there could be. "You write for a skin magazine, too?"

She pushed his shoulder and he fell over onto his back. She wriggled up onto his chest and looked down at him, her hair tickling the sides of his face. "You wish. This is serious."

"Tell me."

For a moment she just looked into his eyes, and the fortune-teller's voice whispered in his memory. *Be clear about what's important to you...*

"I love you, you know," she said, as if he should have known it all along. "As long as we're liberating skeletons from closets, you should know about that one."

A depth charge of emotion went off somewhere under his ribs. If this had been a movie, great rings of atomic pressure would be radiating out from the two of them, changing everything in its path.

*Change is a process, not an event.*

You're wrong, he told the fortune-teller. Sometimes just a few words can close one chapter and open another.

When Lauren had walked away, he'd realized that if he didn't act, he would lose something so precious it couldn't be calculated using bottom lines and financial projections. He had realized that she was worth taking a chance for, worth exposing his inner vulnerabilities for.

Worth taking on her mother and sisters single-handed for.

"I'm not very good at words, you know," he told her. "That's what started this whole thing. I hate talking on the phone. I do most of my communicating by e-mail. I write articles because trying to say what I feel out loud is impossible. I suppose growing up in the same house with Dad is partly responsible for that."

"Is this a roundabout way of letting me down easy?" she demanded. "Because if it is, you can kiss seeing my period underwear goodbye."

"No." It was hard to laugh with her lying on top of him, so he settled for a smile. "It's a roundabout way of saying that if you want a flowery speech about how I feel right now, you'll have to let me get up so I can send you an e-mail."

"Not a chance. And that is so not true. Know what made me fall for you, besides your beautiful dimples and deep dark eyes?"

"The size of my package?"

"That, too. It was the way you talk to me during sex. When it comes right down to just you and me, Josh, you have no problem at all with words."

He smiled up at her. "So here's a word problem for you. One lock plus one key equals what?"

She thought for a moment, then lowered her head and kissed him with such sensuous sweetness he thought he would die of it. When she was finished turning his brain into mush and his body into six feet of rock-hard demand, she raised her head and looked him in the eyes.

"That equals one happy woman who's no longer on the market. Unavailable. Taken."

His smile widened into a grin. "No longer on the loose?"

"Oh, I wouldn't go that far." Her answering smile was full of sin and promise. "Now, do you want to see my period underwear or not?"

# *21*

To: lauren_massey@leftcoastmag.com
From: josh_mccrae@leftcoastmag.com
Re: Congrats

I know I told you this last night, and again in staff meeting in front of everyone else, but this is the official copy. It's an e-mail; it must be real, right? :)

Congrats on landing the *Left Coast* blog. Joanie says she can't wait to get started on your Web site. I'm leaning on Personnel to get your signing bonus through ASAP. There have to be some perks to go with that 33 percent.

I know you can handle reporting and blogging for both mags. In fact, I don't think there's anything you can't do. That's one of the reasons why I love you.

Yours—J.

If you enjoyed what you just read,
then we've got an offer you can't resist!

# Take 2 bestselling love stories FREE!
# Plus get a FREE surprise gift!

The world's bestselling romance series.

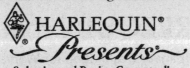

# HARLEQUIN®
## *Presents*

**Seduction and Passion Guaranteed!**

Legally wed, but he's never said...
"I love you."

They're...

*Wedlocked!*

The series
where
marriages are
made in haste...
and love
comes later...

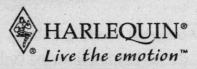

# HARLEQUIN®
## *Live the emotion*™

**www.eHarlequin.com**

HPWL

# An Invitation for Love

## hot tips

Find a special way to invite your guy into your Harlequin Moment. Letting him know you're looking for a little romance will help put his mind on the same page as yours. In fact, if you do it right, he won't be able to stop thinking about you until he sees you again!

Send him a long-stemmed rose tied to an invitation that leaves a lot up to the imagination.

♥

Autograph a favorite photo of you and tape it on the appointed day in his day planner. Block out the hours he'll be spending with you.

♥

Send him a local map and put an *X* on the place you want him to meet you. Write: "I'm lost without you. Come find me. Tonight at 8." Use magazine cutouts and photographs to paste images of romance and the two of you all over the map.

♥

Send him something personal that he'll recognize as yours to his office. Write: "If found, please return. Owner offers reward to anyone returning item by 7:30 on Saturday night." Don't sign the card.

# Harlequin on Location

## hot tips

Wherever your dream date location,
pick a setting and a time that won't be
interrupted by your daily responsibilities.
This is a special time together. Here are
a few hopelessly romantic settings to
inspire you—they might as well be ripped
right out of a Harlequin romance novel!

### Bad weather can be so good.

Take a walk together after a fresh snowfall or when it's just stopped
raining. Pick a snowball (or a puddle) fight, and see how long it takes
to get each other soaked to the bone. Then enjoy drying off in front of
a fire, or perhaps surrounded by lots and lots of candles with yummy
hot chocolate to warm things up.

### Candlelight dinner for two...in the bedroom.

Romantic music and candles will instantly transform the place you
sleep into a cozy little love nest, perfect for nibbling. Why not lay
down a blanket and open a picnic basket at the foot of your bed? Or
set a beautiful table with your finest dishes and glowing candles to set
the mood. Either way, a little bubbly and lots of light finger foods will
make this a meal to remember.

### A Wild and Crazy Weeknight.

Do something unpredictable...on a weeknight straight from work.
Go to an art opening, a farm-team baseball game, the local playhouse,
a book signing by an author or a jazz club—anything but the humdrum
blockbuster movie. There's something very romantic about being
a little wild and crazy—or at least out of the ordinary—that will
bring out the flirt in both of you. And you won't be able to resist
thinking about each other in anticipation of your hot date...or telling
everyone the day after.

# Looking for a seductive cocktail?

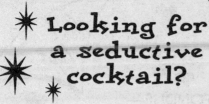

*hot tips*

## Try *Ero-Desiac*— a dazzling martini

With its warm apricot walls yet cool atmosphere, Verlaine is quickly becoming one of New York's hottest nightspots. Verlaine created a light, subtle yet seductive martini for Harlequin: the Ero-Desiac. Sake warms the heart and soul, while jasmine and passion fruit ignite the senses....

## The Ero-Desiac

*Combine vodka, sake, passion fruit puree and jasmine tea. Mix and shake. Strain into a martini glass, then rest pomegranate syrup on the edge of the martini glass and drizzle the syrup down the inside of the glass.*

# Are you a chocolate lover?

*hot tips*

## Try WALDORF CHOCOLATE FONDUE—
a true chocolate decadence

While many couples choose to dine out on Valentine's Day, one of the most romantic things you can do for your sweetheart is to prepare an elegant meal—right in the comfort of your own home.

Harlequin asked John Doherty, executive chef at the Waldorf-Astoria Hotel in New York City, for his recipe for seduction—the famous Waldorf Chocolate Fondue....

## WALDORF CHOCOLATE FONDUE
### Serves 6-8

2 cups water
½ cup corn syrup
1 cup sugar
8 oz dark bitter chocolate, chopped
1 pound cake (can be purchased in supermarket)
2–3 cups assorted berries
2 cups pineapple
½ cup peanut brittle

Bring water, corn syrup and sugar to a boil in a medium-size pot. Turn off the heat and add the chopped chocolate. Strain and pour into fondue pot. Cut cake and fruit into cubes and 1-inch pieces. Place fondue pot in the center of a serving plate, arrange cake, fruit and peanut brittle around pot. Serve with forks.